Alison of the Skies

Mike & family

I hope you enjoy this magical story. I miss you guys!

— C. L. Cameron

11-21-16

C. C. Cameron

This is a work of fiction. All characters and events portrayed in this novel are either fictitious or used fictitiously.

ALISON OF THE SKIES

Copyright © 2016, C. C. Cameron

All rights reserved. Reproduction in part or in whole is strictly forbidden without the express written consent of the publisher.

Cover and interior design by Roseanna White Designs
Cover images from Shutterstock.com
Edited by Donna Garrett

ISBN: 9780692800102

*To the teachers throughout my life.
Thank you for your mentorship and inspiration.*

A LEAP OF FAITH

Everything felt desolate and looking down at the shadows...It was the opposite. Alison gripped the stone wall behind her. The sharp stone grazed the palm of her hand, but she ignored the pain. *"Well, how about that, just a little more,"* she whispered out loud and felt the current of the breeze carry a serene echo. *"This time, the bridge is mine for the taking,"* she uttered in determination as her hands were cold from the night chill, but Alison was moments away from her one potential goal.

The ledge beneath her feet was made of a thin and fragile wood that creaked every time she stepped in the center. *"Here goes nothing...for the tenth time,"* Alison told herself as she prepared for the jump that would hopefully be her first leap to many undetected and desired adventures.

"Aaah!" Alison yelled as her foot slipped and she quickly put her palm to her mouth to hide any more noise. With the other hand she held on to the citadel wall and didn't dare to look back at her bedroom window she had just escaped.

"No retreat...there's no going back empty handed this time." She tried to encourage herself more than ever before. She wasn't going to let her fear of heights get to her this time. Yet she kept gazing down at the dark grassy plain below the citadel. *"Great, now all I need is a bit of luck,"* she said to herself as if it were her last words.

Alison leaped through the air and to her amazement the wind was at her back and gave her the wings of luck. She landed on a small pillar on the bridge of the citadel. She remained still and listened for anyone who might have heard her landing as her heart beat kicked around in her chest from the excitement. This was like taking footsteps of a giant, and the feeling that everything was at stake this time clouded her mind.

Every second that went by she contemplated making a run for it, but restrained herself from moving knowing she could be easily spotted. *"Goodbye mother, it's about time I leave these ruins,"* Alison said under her breath and used every word with rage to push herself to make the run. Off she went darting like a predator in the night. The bridge wasn't helpful as it made rigorous echoing by the swift pounding of her feet. *"Almost at the tree line,"* Alison thought. The citadel itself was in quite a bit of shade as the nearby hill hid the glow of the nightfall moon. The hill was steep and the forest upon it was forbidden to any, but tonight this was Alison's rescue.

Just as she reached the hallway across the bridge, she was spotted. "Hey you! Stop where you are!" the citadel guard yelled out.

Alison didn't dare look back. She tried holding her scarf together as the wind attempted to uncoil it, but her long dark hair still fluttered in the wind as she ran. "He's on the run, don't let 'em reach the tree line!" the same guard yelled to the other citadel soldiers as they ran out onto the bridge.

Alison underestimated them, *"what fools"* she thought, but her patience parted and she picked up her speed.

"Keep your aim on 'em!" The guard in command ordered and three soldiers pulled back their bows and pointed the tip of their arrows right on Alison.

She was almost off the bridge and her heart sank from the dead silence that overcame the moment. She stopped in her tracks briefly and turned an eye on the archers on the other side of the bridge. Without a second to react a gust of wind blew her scarf away and she quickly used her arms to hide her face.

"It's you..." the command guard whispered to himself. "Put em down!" he hollered as he ran to the archers and shoved their bows out of their hands. He called off any from going after her and when he looked back across to the end of the bridge, Alison was gone.

"*Good luck to you...Saves me the trouble...*" the guard whispered under his breath. "Get back to your posts and forget what you saw, it's not our concern," he ordered as he paced back toward the citadel holding his shoulders high with an ego for pride. The commander went back inside the citadel and brushed dust off his shoulder plates and shined his armor, still trying to not care about seeing the queen's daughter run away. "*You stupid girl...it's only a matter of time,*" he said to himself and his words echoed down the long corridor of the citadel. He then trudged out and back to the bridge with an evil grin on his face.

He had no sooner reached his station then he heard loud footsteps coming his way and stood still as he recognized who it was. "Where has she gone this time! I want her found!" the queen shouted as she appeared in front of the guard. He took a gulp as sweat streaked down his forehead as his nerves raged. "Your highness... she has run off into the forest. I have already anticipated she's on the run towards Armsdale." The queen moved closer to the commander and her anger only got worse. "Do what you have to, but bring her back...I'll lock her up in the tower if it means keeping her from running."

The queen said nothing more as she sharply turned away and walked off. "Your highness with your permission I..."

But before he could ask, the queen interrupted, "I said do what you have to...that's my order."

The commanding guard stormed back to the bridge and glared across to the tree line. "This is all too familiar," he said aloud with a bitter tone.

The hill was steep and the wet limestone beneath the earth made it nearly impossible for Alison to go about. *"Well it's done...I'm finished with the likes of this place,"* she told herself as she stopped to catch her breath and lean her back up against a nearby tree. The woods around were dark; her only light was from the full moon above and the stars in the sky. The tall timber trees creaked and the branches rustled in harmony with the wind which caused a cold chill to run up Alison's spine taunting every nerve in her body. *"Well, you don't frighten me,"* Alison bravely said aloud, looking in all directions, but hadn't thought this far in her plan, nor had she ever been to this forbidden place.

"Move Alison, pick a direction," she told herself, growing even more impatient to get far away from the citadel. Without giving it much more thought, she took off into the gloomy forest, but she soon discovered it was quite a dense thicket. Alison was now panicking this time. She was blind to the darkened brush surrounding her. *"Ouch,"* she muttered out multiple times as the vines

and twigs left swelling lacerations on her legs. Her wool coat was slowly, but surely being torn to shreds and the strands of her long dark hair were being snagged by the limbs scratching across her face.

"At this rate I'll be dead meat before getting to Armsdale," she said as she tried to determine the path that would lead her to the small town within the kingdom. The hill became steeper as she went on, her legs were now aching from the climb and her ankles felt like they were on the brink of collapse.

Alison was now at the highest point she could find. The moon above her cast light on her surroundings and in the distance lights, like fireflies, glowed against the night. *"There, now I just need to..."* Alison stopped short of her whisper. The tree tops above bent forward as if a gust was pulling them down. A gigantic object raced above the trees, breaking branches and sending them like shards of glass toward Alison.

She fell back after tripping over a root, but paid no attention to her fall as she, herself, was in complete awe. The giant swayed through the forest trees as the sound of cracking wood fibers were carried on the haunted wind. She watched as it drifted away toward Armsdale. *"What was that!"* Alison thought to herself. The mood of the surrounding forest suddenly became quiet and mysterious.

Before she could get back on her feet she felt like

eyes were set on her and in that moment a howl from the distance caught her attention and sent a chill up her spine. She really wanted to get out of there, but which way to go? She pulled herself up by the tree branches, began looking around as she was trying to get her direction. *"Thank goodness. Armsdale, that way,"* she said aloud, and took off running like a wolf in the night, momentum pumping through her veins far greater than ever before.

Unfortunately, the hill was steep and her feet took on a mind of their own, flying faster and faster as she was being slapped and scratched by branches while at the same time the soft turf was making it hard to keep her balance, especially in the dark. She was trying to grab hold of the branches to steady herself, but before she could react her dark leather shoes got caught in the muck and slipped off of her feet, and with her rapid downhill momentum she found herself taking a short flight through the branches and landing face down on the forest floor - without her shoes...

"Just what I needed, now what!" Alison yelled in a frustrated manner. She felt unbalanced and her stability became weak. *"Here I go, I'm okay, I'm just out of breath..."* she thought and before she could crawl back to get her shoes the slope beneath her collapsed partially and sent Alison rolling like a tumbleweed all the way to the bottom. Injured with cuts and scrapes, Alison held

pressure on her legs to hide the pain. *"I'm going to be in Armsdale in pieces at this rate..."* she muttered to herself while looking at the torn tunic she had borrowed from the citadel. Seeing the way she looked made her miss the feeling of looking like a girl of royalty. Alison sat in silence for a few moments fearing what else lay ahead to stop her short of her destination. Then she broke off a long, thin branch from a tree above her and used it to balance her steps, determined to move forward. Soon she came to the end of the forest and could see Armsdale in full view. Never before had Alison been able to leave the citadel, not even to visit the towns within the area. *"Here at last,"* she thought, wiping sweat from her forehead.

The night was young and the journey so far had made Alison quite weary, but she knew sunrise was still very distant. She hurried to the border and when she saw how pathetic the fence was around the perimeter of the town, she knew there would be no problem getting in. Alison was shoeless and her pants and tunic, like those of the tower guards, were worn out with holes everywhere. She did, however, use her scarf to her advantage, which by some miracle was still intact, so she wrapped it around her face and hoped she didn't make a scene, but rather just looked like a lonely refugee. Armsdale was far from quiet. As Alison walked through the paved alleyways she could hear music playing in the distance and laughter from something entertaining in the town square.

Alison stopped to think as she crossed her arms against her chest and could feel the chilling wind once again. She kept her head down low as she walked closer and closer to the happy commotion. Suddenly a carriage pulled by a trotting horse came down the street toward her. She swiftly moved over to a corner of a shop and placed her head against the wall hoping the shadows would keep her hidden. "Say young lady, are you lost if you don't mind me asking?" came a voice as the horses stopped in their tracks. Alison didn't answer at first as she could not see the man's face. "It's quite chilly out tonight, here take this," the man said as he threw a jacket to Alison. She watched it slowly fall to the ground and did not react.

"Find her, we have our orders!" came a loud voice from the square. The crowd of people panicked and left the streets as citadel guards marched through quickly, disrupting the whole seen.

"They found me already? They're quick," Alison said aloud.

The man sitting in the carriage turned his head toward Alison and his face showed slightly in the moonlight. "It's a full moon tonight. There's not enough shadow to hide. Get in. I'll keep you hidden," the stranger said as he pulled a latch and a small door came open. Alison gazed in and even thought it was a cramped space, to her judgment she knew she had to take the chance. So she dove forward and squeezed to fit. The door closed behind her and the man on top of the carriage ordered the horses to move.

"Keep searching, she can't be too far from here, there's no way she got past Armsdale this quickly on foot." Alison heard the same voice from a guard, only this time they were getting closer. The stranger hiding Alison tightened the cloth around his face and pulled his hat down to the point only his eyes could be seen. "Stop there, mister…I said hold!" a guard shouted as more of them appeared and surrounded the carriage. The stranger ordered his horses to halt.

"And what can I do for you, captain?" he asked.

"We're searching your carriage. We have orders to find a young lady. She's from the royal family and tonight she's a little escape artist."

"Ah, I see. Well I can assure you, you won't find her here."

"And who are you? You don't sound like you're from anywhere around."

The stranger darted a stare at the guard. "Nobody important, just passing through."

The leader looked away and reached for the door of the carriage. "Wrong answer, pal," the guard said in a frustrated voice.

"Wait now, like I said, I haven't seen any girl around here," the stranger said raising his voice. Again the guard tried to open the latch.

"This is your final straw, like I said...there...I have not come across...any," the stranger paused as a loud creaking followed as the door flew open and the guard was thrown onto his back. Alison's leg hung out as the carriage sped away. "Now that's what I call a kick!" the stranger yelled back to Alison. They turned hard right and raced down a narrow alleyway.

"He's got her! After the girl and bring me the riders head!" yelled the guard as he was lifting himself up and back onto his feet. The soldiers did not hesitate and they each charged in the direction the two had fled.

"Hang on! I'll lose them!" the stranger called back to Alison who was still squished against many random objects. She wasn't paying attention to the stranger; her mind was set on getting back into the dark alleys.

"Look, tell me where we are going. I'm the one they're after and they have their orders and will stop at nothing!" Alison yelled back. The carriage swiftly made sharp turns and Alison was thrown around like a ragdoll as they raced through the plaza. The stranger slowed down the horses as they reached a dead end where a large brick wall stood in their way. The stranger, guiding the horses, looked back as he saw the open door swinging back and forth and Alison was gone. *"Good luck going that route,"* he said to himself. The soldiers now on horseback reached the horse and carriage only to find it abandoned and Alison and the stranger were nowhere to be found.

The pavement was slick as the dew dripped off the trees above. Alison knew the moon was almost at horizon and sunrise was about to make its presence. *"Hide Alison...hide,"* she thought. She knew she could never make it out of Armsdale without being caught in the daylight. Alison, now nearly out of breath, stopped in her path wondering which way to turn. The town markets all around hid her as if she was in a labyrinth, but it was only a matter of time before someone recognized her.

She didn't think too much about the stranger from before. As time passed, her only thoughts were *"Escape."* As she stood there, looking around, from the corner of her eye Alison spotted a small run-down market. She didn't think twice about taking shelter there for her own advantage. Inside the smell was musty and the curtains barely hanging from the windows swayed like waves with the crisp breeze. *"Looks like a shipwreck in here,"* Alison thought to herself as she went up the stairs and into the loft above.

Suddenly she heard a noise that sounded all too familiar. The sound of heavy footsteps approached from outside and Alison wondered how she was found so easily. She considered climbing out the window, but she was not fond of heights and abandoned that thought. She ran to the only window in the room and to her surprise the drop wasn't as frightening as she had thought. But there was this large hole down below and looking down from the window Alison wasn't so sure what she was looking into.

The footsteps turned from a small echo into a thundering stomp and Alison was shaking inside and hesitated to go any further. She stood on the tips of her toes, to slowly walk across the ledge of the window and stretched every step she could to be nowhere near the room. The morning was now quickly coming and the still quietness of the town ruined her concentration. *"Where is he now...?"* Alison whispered under the heavy breaths she was taking as if her heart frantically skipped beats.

Alison suddenly lost balance as a shadow shaped like an armed guard appeared on the outside wall. Her sight faded to darkness and all sound seized after the crash.

DREAMS OF SUNRISE

The petals drifted as the wind at her back swept them in her current. Angels flew down from the heavens above and she did not fear. They were loyal to her and on their way down one pulled out a lustrous golden crown. Each came to the ground bowed before Alison. The one with the crown approached her and placed the crown upon her head. Then came singing accompanied by lyres ringing a tune that could be heard for miles. Standing in her field of dreams Alison reached her arms up in supplication and wished for the night sky, and suddenly, before she knew it, the magic of night descended. The stars twinkled as did her eyes. She was her own star and tonight she was queen. Tears crept slowly down her cheeks and a jolt of sanctity ran through her veins. They were tears of joy and Alison never felt so happy. Alison called to the angels behind her, and as she turned to them she discovered they were no longer there. In their place was one particular star in the sky. As she watched in wonder and awe it seemed to come closer and closer, until she just wanted to reach up and touch it. Its radiant beauty seized the night and certainly captivated her attention. The more she gazed at the star, the closer it seemed to be moving towards her. Then suddenly Alison realized the star was falling straight for the land. Swiftly she sought escape but there was no place to hide, and she called for it to come to a halt. The star slowed down and everything became dead silent. The light from the star grew intensely until a flash struck the air. The star corrupted into falling embers of light and struck the land around. *"No!"* Alison screamed. She gave commands, yelling them at the top of her lungs, but instead the ground shook as the pieces continued falling. The meadow and all the beauty around turned to ash as the flames scorched the land. *"No, wait!"* Alison cried out again and fell to her knees. None of the pieces struck her, but inside she was shattered. She felt like little broken pieces of glass being stepped on by all the people who ever looked down upon her.

What really took her breath away was that she had closed her eyes in fear and when she opened them she realized she was finally awake with the rays of the sun gleaming through the cracks and reflecting off Alison's eyes. Confusion sank in her gut and she was perplexed with wondering where exactly she was. It was cramped for sure, even worse than the carriage from before. Alison put her eye to one of the larger cracks and moved her hands around to feel what she was in. The barrier around felt soft like a sea shell and a shadow moving back and forth kept her view limited. "Enough!" Alison shouted as she suddenly stood up and emerged from the darkness. The lid shattered in pieces and Alison was bewildered to find herself rising out of a large urn. It was as if she rose from the dead and puzzled back in reality.

"Well, well, you're finally awake...that was quite entertaining," came a calm and exquisite male voice. Alison was startled at the voice that sounded familiar and she looked around to see who it was.

"Wha...woah!" she yelled holding onto the edge as the urn tipped over and crashed onto the floor. The timber below her feet creaked as she struggled to stand. Her sight was foggy but she could see a person walking toward her as a hand reached out to help. But Alison backed away as she attempted to recover from her dizziness as confusion sunk in when she realized she was back indoors.

"You'll be fine if you can stay still for once. Looks like you've been running since we ditched the carriage."

It took her a few moments, but after coming back to reality, she was stunned by the boy in front of her. "You... that was you back there?" Alison mumbled as she was lost for words and couldn't help but focus on his dark blue tunic and an old strand of rope tied at his waist.

"You caused quite a scene back there. You must have really done something to upset those soldiers," the boy replied.

Alison, now staring into his aqua blue eyes, was in awe and she was slightly blushing from his charm. She twitched her hand as she had the urge to move. "So you left me in this urn after I fell? Great so now I've been kidnapped," Alison said in a sarcastic tone hoping she got her point across.

"Yep, I managed to witness your little fall there. Thankfully no one else noticed a little girl falling out of second story window. Anyways, I brought you back inside and put that lid on to keep you undiscovered and asleep for the time being. But I must say, you sure talk more in your sleep," the stranger said and chuckled a little.

Alison was between annoyed and confused and her head hurt to much to think of her latest plan. "So who are you, stranger? You're not from around here."

"What makes you say that?" the stranger quickly asked. He stepped closer toward Alison, who still not trusting him, was backing away but then found that she had backed herself right into a corner. She was nearly in a panic. What to do next? Try to run past this stranger out into the street? But if she did that, she would surely be caught. She still couldn't figure out where they were, but wherever it was, it was small and vacant. As the stranger turned his face to a window, the moonlight revealed that he was not much older than herself, if at all. The strange boy's eyes now sparkled like stars and Alison started to blush. She knew deep inside he was definitely not from around here and she thought how peculiar it was that he was in her presence.

"I think I'll be on my way. I've already wasted much precious time," Alison spoke softly to him. She really meant to sound more rushed for time, but she was still in awe.

"Well, if you think I'm stopping you then you're mistaken," he told her.

Alison looked at her only exit, the door behind him that was halfway open. She shifted her focus, but remained confused on plans to move onward. She craved some fresh air or any excuse to escape while it was dark. "Guess I'll be going now..." Alison hesitated, then stepped forward with determination. It was then when she realized she wasn't wearing her own coat before, but still had the citadel tunic on. Her sleeve brushed against the stranger as she passed by him and strangely he just stood there with his head turned downward. She looked one last time, to get a good look at his face, but the room was just too dark. As she continued on, just before reaching the doorway she felt a hand on her shoulder and she stopped suddenly in her tracks. She gazed down at some pointed brown boots that made her feel like she was now in the presence of a very…very strange outsider. "Look mister, I told you…"

"And I'm telling you, you won't make it a quarter of the way through town. You're too noticeable," came the strange boy's voice in a whisper as he stood behind her. He slowly took his hand off her shoulder and stepped back.

"You're worried I'm too noticeable? Look who's talking. People around here would wonder if you're even from Earth," Alison said to him and grinned like she had won a fight.

"And I would tell them…no…I am not," he replied.

Alison quickly dropped her grin as if she was being played for a fool. "I think I've seen and obviously heard enough of this for one day. I guess I hit my head harder than…" before Alison could finish, the boy swiftly turned around and motioned for her to be silent. He walked over to the one window in the room and flung it open. The curtains twirled as the crisp wind came through and the light of the moon now enhanced the entire room. "Hear that? Sounds like your search party is still at it," he said looking back at her. She was confused as she heard nothing more than the howling of dogs in the distance. "Come with me. I can get you where you really want to be," the strange boy said as he put out his hand for her to grasp. Alison didn't take him seriously and instead of replying she fought to hold back a laugh as she focused on his unordinary shoes.

"I have..." Alison paused before finishing what she had to say; she was interrupted by those familiar footsteps again.

"There's no time. Come with me," the boy whispered urgently and without thinking it through she agreed and took his hand. They raced out the door and up a long flight of stairs. "You're about to take a leap of faith again, only this time you won't be falling into an urn; that I can promise," he said and showed a quick grin. Alison struggled to think clearly especially after hearing he was there to witness her fall from before. They reached the second floor and before Alison could stop from running off the balcony before her, the boy seized her by the waist and took a giant leap into open air. Alison, who was terrified, prepared for a great fall, but it never came. She closed her eyes tightly and struggled to keep her tears at bay, but with every emotion at stake she let them fall. "You really are beautiful, aren't you?" the boy said, more a statement than a question. Alison was breathless and for a moment she was at a loss for words. She blushed again and felt as if she took a leap into a fairy tale. "Hang on tight; this part is harsh for beginners," he said as he held onto Alison with one hand and grasped a ladder with the other hand.

"Where are we? What's going on?!" she yelled out loud. The night air was so serene and the town of Armsdale down below became smaller as the ladder slowly moved upward in the sky. Alison felt a small feeling of butterflies in her stomach and she didn't know what to say. She was in a state where all possible words to describe what was happening were lost.

CHAPTER 3

ONWARD JOURNEY

Alison, now puzzled as ever before, not knowing if she was still in a dream or if this was real. The sun's light erupted the morning, with shards of rays shining through the clouds. "How is this possible and where is this taking us?" Alison demanded to know and, after all, the heights were releasing her fears.

"It's best that I show you, I can't imagine you will be too surprised in the end." Of course Alison was utterly curious and showed no animosity to the situation. She tried to relax her mind and her body actually felt comfortable sitting on the rope ladder. "You're of royalty I presume. I can't even imagine how you feel." He was right though and Alison didn't even question his assumption of her being from royalty even though it was true. "Ah, where are my manners? I am Dante by the way...Dante of the Skies" he said to Alison who was holding on just below him.

She could now get a better view of this boy, Dante, and she noticed a small gold chain that hung from his pocket. Again she stared at his ridiculous-looking pair of shoes that were pointed and curved upward. "Why are you here? And where are you taking me anyways?" Alison asked more calmly this time.

"Altaria is my home and since you want to know so badly, we're going up to my sky ship. It's a long way up and I do apologize for the time it's taking."

"You really expect me to believe you're taking me to a ship?" Alison muttered as if she was talking to an idiot.

"Actually, yes. I climbed down from the ship to Earth and quite frankly I think it's the best way to have gotten there."

"Falling out of the sky sounds silly enough, but if you're telling me you actually climbed down from the sky then you're just crazy."

Dante grinned upon hearing this. "Well, if you don't believe me then I can't imagine what theory you have for this ladder going upwards, look just how high up we are!" Alison looked down to where Armsdale was, but they were so high up all she could see were the clouds rolling by.

"Oh great, so now there's a ship and let me guess, it floats in the sky and that's why you call yourself Dante of the Skies. How stupid do you think I am?"

"Actually I think you're pretty smart, but what, you've never seen a sky ship? What kind of place is this Earth? What a boring place."

Before Alison could say another word, Dante grabbed her hand and she felt a jolt and tug as he hoisted her up and over the side of the ship and Dante went after. Alison and Dante landed softly on solid ground. "You can open your eyes now," said Dante. "Don't be afraid, Alison," Dante said encouraging her. Alison thought to herself, *"It's only a dream, it's only just a dream."* And also she couldn't recall telling Dante her name. She finally opened her eyes to find herself upon the deck of a great big ship. Alison was in greater awe than ever before and was filled with excitement and wonder.

"It's a whole new world when you look at it from up here," Dante said and made it sound like this was the true meaning of freedom. *But who was he really? And where did he come from?* Alison thought as she struggled with believing this was all real. But it had to be. Didn't it? Because, after all, she was standing on a ship in the sky. *"But how is this happening to me? And could I really leave home just like this?"* Alison's heart sank and she had to remind herself, *"It's just a dream and I'll wake up any moment now."*

CHAPTER 4

THE STARRY NIGHT

Alison's hair blew sideways across her face as the wind passed through each strand. The ship swayed in all directions, but Alison felt safe because Dante held her tightly as they walked together across the deck. They had got so far up in the sky that they passed through the clouds like ghosts. Alison, still fearing the height, was awestruck. "I questioned what I was thinking by actually trusting you, but after seeing this, I'm so glad I did. I can't believe this is happening!" Alison felt the freedom; whether it would only last a minute or forever, she was actually away from home and in the back of her mind enjoyed the feeling that she had found the great escape.

The wind currents were stronger now and took her

breath away. "I really must be dreaming, I'm on a ship in the sky."

"Not just any ship," Dante corrected her.

Alison was amazed, but she thought if this were a dream then this was by far the most exotic one ever.

"I guess down on your turf, you and your people have never seen a sky ship."

"No, the only ones I've ever seen were the ships my father sailed at sea," Alison explained. She was now both frantic and amazed. "I thought you were crazy when you said we were going up to a ship in the sky, but now not only do I think you're crazy, but…" Alison couldn't finish speaking as she tried to take it all in.

"You're now aboard 'The Majesty.' Let's just say I borrowed it from Altaria.

"Altaria," Alison wondered. She looked over the side of the ship and couldn't even see the ground below. Home was now gone and Alison was lost in the sky. Dante was still a stranger, but somehow she didn't feel afraid of him, and the only thing that urged her to keep exploring was the fact that he had been right; Alison had found the escape she desired, he had made it possible, even more amazing than her wildest imagination. Alison gave Dante a stare and asked, "How is this all real?"

"What do you mean, how is this real?"

Alison looked all around in wonder. "The ship… floating in mid-air."

He walked over and put his hand on Alison's shoulder. "Saphyres," he said. "It's the crystal mineral my people harvest. It grows in the core of Altaria and we harness its power." Alison looked at him in a daze, but then nodded like she understood every word he said. "You may be amazed now, Alison, but come with me to Altaria and I'll show you truly incredible beauty." Alison stood quietly, but then turned to him as he awaited an answer.

"How long will it take for us to arrive?" Alison asked.

"With a sky ship, we will be at the city of Altaria in no time." Dante took her by the hand once again and led her up wooden stairs onto the upper deck. There was the ship's wheel and Dante took hold of it, standing with a proud posture. He looked like a true hero and Alison wondered if her dreams were really coming true after all.

"So Dante, Captain of the Skies...now that has a nice ring to it." Alison said and gave a smile to Dante. He stood still staring into her eyes and tried holding back a laugh. "Here, I'm sure this will suit your taste," Dante said as he left the wheel and walked over to a nearby chest and pulled out a very elegant dress from a chest beside him. The dress danced in the wind as he held it up to her. It was a crimson red and had small crystals dangling from it that shined in the light. Alison gazed at the dress and wondered why he had a dress on his ship. "You're probably wondering why I have this... Well, normally a ship like this has a crew..." Dante said and quickly tried to save himself of the embarrassment of having a dress on his ship. "I figured it wouldn't take long before you got tired of the ragged clothes on your back," he explained. Alison reached out and took it, still amazed by its beauty. He motioned for her to go below deck to change and when she came back to the surface, it was Dante who was in awe this time. "Marvelous," he whispered.

"You knew this whole time, didn't you?" she asked.

"Knew what exactly?" Dante replied and smiled.

"That I was going to come away with you this whole time?"

"I don't know what you're talking about," Dante said, still admiring her beauty. Alison had washed away the dirt and marks from her skin while below deck and her hair matched perfectly with her dress and for once she felt like true royalty.

"You mentioned saphyres and said the saphyres bestows energy to your people," Alison said as she looked into Dante's eyes.

"That's correct. Like I said, it grows at the core of Altaria."

Alison wondered why the mineral was so significant, but then it came to her and she realized the possible truth. "So that's how we are sailing, or rather floating; the ship has this mineral you speak of powering it?"

"That's exactly correct. The saphyres is no ordinary

crystal mineral." As they sailed through the clouds, she was intrigued by the saphyres he spoke of. "Would you like to see it?" Dante asked, as if he knew that Alison was too shy to ask.

"Of course!" Alison replied. The journey had just begun, but in that moment it felt as if they had been sailing along for ages. Her ambition was growing as Alison yearned to discover this "Altaria" Dante spoke of.

Dante took Alison all over the ship, its structure and shape was quite impressive. They went far below deck until they were in a very dark room. "Put these on," said Dante as he handed Alison a pair of odd-looking glasses. Dante walked over to a small iron handle on the left wall. He lifted the switch and slowly a small door opened. Now she knew why she needed these goggles in this darkened room, for the whole room was suddenly illuminated by a brilliant, blinding radiance of light from the saphyres.

"It's beautiful," Alison whispered as a sense of joy lifted her. When the door was all the way opened, the entire crystal of saphyres was in sight. It was a shiny lime green crystal, the size of a melon. It was held by iron bars to keep it in place. Dante explained that the energy from the saphyres is so strong that it defies the laws of gravity.

Alison thought intensely, "But how then are we..."

Dante interrupted, "I knew you were going to ask. The reason we aren't floating ourselves is because of these." Dante pointed at the small iron bars surrounding the crystal. "These bars allow the energy to flow down them and all around the hull of the ship, allowing it to float. We remain standing because of these bars. They block the energy from affecting us while still collecting energy and sending it through the ship. The energy from this mineral is the verything that gives my people the ability to thrive. Without it, everything would come crashing down."

Alison sighed, "Well, it is amazing and I've never seen anything like it"

"Just wait 'til you see Altaria," replied Dante and before Alison could say another word, Dante took her hand and swiftly led her back up the stairs. Out on the deck the daylight was slowly setting and the sun appeared like a giant phoenix, turning the sky orange. Dante took Alison up another flight of stairs to the captain's deck.

Alison ran over to the ship's wheel. "Look who's king of the skies now!" Alison laughed as she grabbed the helm.

"Careful now, we don't want to go too far off course," Dante said. For the first time in Alison's life, she felt like a queen, but most importantly she was free – free! And nothing was going to stop that. Suddenly, once again Alison felt butterflies in her stomach. Not because of the excitement in the air, but because of the warmth of

Dante as he stood behind her and placed his hands on hers steering the ship and going places few have ever gone before. She continued to look into his eyes and his caring touch dazzled her.

    Alison's attention then drifted over to the side of the ship. She swiftly stepped over to the rail and as she leaned out and gazed around she felt the power of grace run through her. Alison was happy, but still she battled against the tide of joy and reality. She contemplated the thousands of thoughts racing all at once. There was such conflict within her from the thoughts of her mother. But instead of dwelling on that and the anxiety that came with it, she laid down on the hard wooden deck, gazing out into the sky, enjoying the clouds as they drifted right through them, and her mind slowly settled in wonder. She must have dozed off because suddenly she opened her eyes to a fading daylight and the cool evening breeze felt so refreshing. She was so relaxed, more relaxed than she had been in a long, long time. In fact, Alison's spirit felt free as a bird. She contemplated why all this was taking place, but as she reclined on the ship's deck she felt that the "why" really didn't matter, she no longer had a care in the world.

    Night came quickly and the breeze turned from cool to frigid. And right about that time she saw Dante coming toward her carrying a blanket. As she gratefully wrapped it around her, Dante stretched out right next to her on the deck. They both laid there staring up in awe at the luminous stars. "Amazing, isn't it," he said.

"The stars are always impressive. Sometimes I look up from my window back home and wonder how something so beautiful can be so far away," Alison replied. Her eyes were glistening as they reflected the light from the heavens above.

"So you like stars, huh?" Dante asked.

"Of course."

"Then how about a better view?" Dante asked.

Alison was confused as she thought to herself, "How can it possibly get better than this?"

Once again Dante took her by the hand and gently led the way. She had left her blanket on the deck and the wind's night chill gave Alison goose bumps, but just the touch of Dante warmed her and she no longer thought about Mother Nature's atmosphere. Her attention was on him and she didn't care where he took her as long as she could stay in his haven. Dante and Alison stopped just short of the very center of the ship, a long wooden pillar towered high up in the sky and the sails fluttered as every gust of air passed. "Up we go," Dante said. His words were full of serenity as if knowing the secret of what was to come. There was a long ladder on the side of the pillar leading up to the top, although the clouds hid the view of where it led.

"The last time I climbed a ladder with you, I found

myself on a magic flying ship and now you expect me to go up another? What's next? Flying elephants?" Alison snickered, with a big smile on her face.

"Well, I don't know about elephants, but I'm sure this will excite you almost as much." There again was that charming way of words Dante expressed. This time Alison didn't blush, she trusted him and together they went further up into the night sky. With every step she took up the ladder Alison spotted more and more flickering lights that reminded her of dancing fireflies. They finally came to the overlook station. "This is the crow's nest," Dante explained. He reached high up and lifted himself upwards and then he was gone.

"Where did you go, I can't just stay down here, the wind is..." Alison lost her words as a hand reached down. She grabbed hold of it and was swiftly hoisted up. She felt she had suddenly emerged into a new dimension. She was totally speechless. Her mind was in awe as her eyes gazed around in all directions. "Wooow, it's amazing, Dante!" Alison then realized it was the first time she had actually spoken his name. This moment was special and Alison couldn't have been happier than to sail away into the night sky right beside him.

"I told you, from up here the world isn't so small after all and just look down there," he told her as he embraced the moment with much enthusiasm.

"I can see the villages below," Alison exclaimed as she

felt like the free bird she had always imagined.

"Alison," Dante said in a calm tone.

"Yes? What is it?"

"I'm glad you're here with me."

Alison paused as if frozen in ice. "Me too, but it's, well..."

"Well, what?"

"It's almost too good to be true."

Dante turned away and placed his hands on the rails of the platform. "You know I've never really given much thought."

"Thought to what?" Alison asked.

"Nothing, it's nothing. Never mind." Alison could since Dante struggled to get a thought off his chest. "Alison you know your spec..."

"Dante what's that coming our way?" Dante darted over to Alison.

In the distance he could see a shape of something much bigger than his ship, The Majesty. "Uh Oh!"

"It looks like a..." Alison didn't finish. Instead she tried her best to make out what was coming at them, but it was still so dark.

"It's a ship," Dante said. His focus remained on the ship ahead, and whoever was on the ship. He was not pleased, Alison could tell that much. "Alison! Come quick we need to turn the rudder and face the sails to the east!" Alison couldn't understand the problem at hand,

and anyway she had totally lost her sense of direction. Which way was east? Before Alison had time to react Dante seized her arm and lifted her onto his back. "Don't worry. We'll be fine. You're too slow moving on a ladder so I'll carry you back down."

"Oh, I'm the slow one, huh?" she chided.

Dante didn't reply. He hopped over the side carrying Alison. He didn't bother climbing down; instead he used the rails of the ladder to his advantage and slid down to the deck. "Alison, I need you to get to the helm and turn the wheel as soon as I say so."

"Right," Alison replied. She knew that whatever decision Dante made he would strive to keep her safe. Alison grabbed hold of the wheel. She used every ounce in her body to keep a firm grip. "Dante, they're gaining up on us!" she screamed.

"Hang on, I'll be right back. I need to tighten the sails." Dante pulled a wooden lever and then forced it immediately left. He took a piece of timber that had broken off and used it to brace the lever from going back into place. "Alison, start to turn the wheel slowly right and when I say so, release the wheel." Alison turned to reply, but she was speechless as she watched Dante climbing up the wooden pillar all the way up to the sail. She couldn't believe his speed and agility. Dante reached the top and with all his strength he tugged the rope towards him and then let it go, all the sails then loosened. "Now Alison!" Dante shouted. The ship had now turned and Alison let go of the wheel. The force was so strong from the turn, Alison lost her balance and fell to the deck. Dante hadn't realized what had happened to her. He pulled the rope once again with all his might and the sail tightened. The current of the wind filled the sail and the ship took off with great speed. "Alison, we did it! There's no way they're going to catch up to us now." He was basking in the moment of pride and accomplishment, but there was no reply from her. "Alison, where are you?" he called. But still no answer. His attention turned to the deck straight below his feet and there was Alison lying on the deck. "Alison!" Dante shouted, he took hold of the rope and swung down. When he landed he raced to her as his heartbeat pounded at his chest. "Alison, are you okay? Say something!" Dante knelt down and held her head up.

Alison then spoke briefly, "Dante did we beat them? Are they gone?" Alison could only whisper, she was hardly conscious.

He peered into the night sky behind them; the ship chasing them had disappeared. "Yes, they're gone. Just hang on a little longer. I know you will be happy when we arrive at Altaria!" Dante tried desperately to keep her hopes up and keep that smile that still continued to widen across her face. Alison closed her eyes slowly, the smile didn't go away, but she was soon unconscious again.

"Alison, I'll get you help. Just hang on, we're almost home." Tears filled his eyes, overflowing until they fell onto Alison's pale face. *"I can't believe this, for once I felt true happiness, and...love,"* Dante uttered to himself. *"It's her, Alison, you will meet her soon. She's the reason for this and I'll make her pay."* Dante struggled to focus, his hands tightened into a fist and a wave of wrath sparked inside him. He then picked up Alison's unconscious body and stormed back to the ladder leading up to the crow's nest. On his way he could hear the wind getting heavier and felt the breeze blowing his hair sideways. Something caught his attention in the corner of his eye, he turned to the left and parallel to him was the ship still in pursuit. Dante was so shocked he almost dropped Alison. *"It is her, my hunch was right,"* he thought to himself. Anger now flamed in his eyes, but his focus remained on keeping Alison safe. Dante ignored the ship and continued on up. But he came to a halt as the woman he intended to flee from scowled at him from the balcony of her own big ship. Dante glared back at her, struggling to keep Alison on his back. "There's no need for this, now leave!" Dante shouted. He stood there still as if time had stopped for the moment. His mind, still full of rage, never took the attention off of the woman. "I'm free now, you can't stop me." Dante felt like shouting again, but could only say the words in a low tone. He closed his eyes, imploring his heart for peace and the moment just went by too fast. When he opened his eyes the enormous ship was gone, clouds rolled in, impairing vision all around. Dante sighed with relief. Sweat and tears together rolled down his cheeks and he knew it was only matter of time before once again he would come face to face with "her." "Alison I'm taking you back up to your favorite place and for the rest of the night we will be with the stars," Dante whispered in her ear, hoping she would somehow hear him and feel a sense of relief and joy. With Alison on his back, he reached the top and placed her on the lookout deck. He then took a blanket and wrapped her in it to keep her warm. The night air was crisp, and as the ship emerged out of the clouds, the moon rays rained above them and the stars twinkled brightly. Dante wished, *"If only Alison could see this, even if it were the last time."* He sat beside her and grinned when he noticed she slowly opened first one eye and then the other.

    She had pulled through and looked like she would be fine. "Dante, are you okay, are we okay?" asked Alison. She started to pull her blanket off, but then quickly snuggled back in it when she realized the air was frigid.

    "Yes, we are, I'm glad to see you're awake. Look at that!" Dante pointed to the sky and there was a beautiful sequence of stars. "Isn't it amazing? In fact it's my favorite constellation." Alison tried to make a smile, but the cold air made her shiver. "Here allow me," Dante said as he wrapped his arms around her. The warmth of Dante's body was like a furnace in the winter. Alison blushed. She was no longer cold, no longer in pain, she was safe and for once Alison could feel love. "Look!" Dante called out. "It's a shooting star."

"Well, make a wish." Alison turned and looked into Dante's dazzling eyes and then turned her attention to the sky.

"Did you make the wish?" asked Dante.

"I sure did."

"Then tell me. What did you wish for?" Dante asked.

Alison smiled and then burst out in laughter. "I'm not telling you," she teased.

"That's no fair. You would have never seen the shooting star, had I not pointed it out," Dante declared as he too laughed.

"That's just how it works. If I tell you then it will never come true."

"Then when will I ever find out?" Dante asked curiously, hoping she would give in.

"That's for me to know and for you to spend hours trying to find out, but failing in the end," Alison teased sarcastically and laughed again.

Dante grinned. "You know, you really are something; actually you're amazing." Alison was speechless. Her cheeks turned red and she hid under the blanket to hide her blush, but acted like she was just cold.

"It's okay, haha, take your time."

Alison sat back up and took the blanket off her face, she leaned into Dante and before she gave Dante time to say anything on his mind, she kissed him on his cheek. "You are my hero, Dante."

This time Dante was the one to blush. "It was nothing." The next few minutes were spent silently, as neither said a word. "You know it's funny..." Dante stopped as he realized Alison had fallen asleep. He smiled and put his arm around her. He closed his eyes and thought to himself, *"We are on top of the world."* The words kept racing through his mind in array. It was true though, they were free as a bird, and there was nothing weighing them down and no one to stop them.

Tonight Alison got her wish, it was finally a dream come true.

HALO

Alison could touch the wings of the butterflies as they danced around her. The wind carried a melody along the current and it made Alison dance too. She twirled and twirled, but never became dizzy. She was in a field and with every step she took more and more flowers blossomed. She walked over to one and picked off the bloom and held it to her face. With a deep breath she inhaled its aroma. One of the butterflies then landed on top of the flower petals. "Well, aren't you just the prettiest little thing," Alison said aloud. She reached her hand out to touch its wings, but the butterfly flew off into the breeze. "Wait, don't go," called Alison as she watched it fly off into the sky. The wind steadily picked up its strength and Alison could feel the current as it blew her hair and dress sideways. Alison noticed the dancing butterflies were gone. *"But where did they go?"* she thought curiously. "Why are the flowers gone too?" Alison shrieked. As she looked down she saw that all the flowers in the field were now dead. Petals lay everywhere and the flower's stems drooped downward as if their very life had been drained from them. The forest trees that bordered the field swayed from left to right as the heavy wind changed in all directions. The wind was so intense Alison lost her balance and fell. Lighting and darkness seized the great blue sky. Strikes came down and before she knew it, the field was in flames. The air around her was scorched and the ashes that landed on Alison's dress ruined it as the fabric slowly burned. Alison's heart raced, she was in a state of horrid fear and just like the wind, she too ran in all directions. She ran as fast as she could toward the tree line, but finally stopped in misery. No matter how fast she ran, she was never any closer to the trees and the flames behind her sparked and crackled as they burned the dead field. The flames came closer and closer! Alison stood trembling until her weak body finally collapsed. She curled her body into a ball and in agony yelled, "Help me, please!" Everything around was haunted, in gloom, and the fire made her feel like she had fallen into the underworld. Alison closed her eyes, tightened up her fists and pounded the ground she was lying on. Tears fell from her eyes, but the scorching heat dried them up before they could fall. With one last breath she gave her heart and mind one last attempt for help or it was all over. "Dante!!!!" Alison screamed.

"What!" came a voice.

"Dante help me!"

"Alison. Wake up!"

"Dante?"

"Alison, wake up!" Dante shook her by the shoulders vigorously, until finally she awoke.

"What? Where am I? What happened?" Alison asked in a confused voice. She looked around and then realized she was still on The Majesty. The moonlight was shining on Alison's face; it showed just how pale her skin was, but to Dante it showed just how beautiful she was.

"Not again, oh, not again," she wept.

"What do you mean?" Dante asked her.

"I was dreaming..."

"Well of course you were. In fact it sounded more like a nightmare."

"Sounded?"

"Well, yes. I mean you kept yelling my name and asking for help, so I shook you until you woke up. And boy, let me tell you, you are you a hard sleeper," he teased.

Alison felt embarrassed and clumsy. "Sorry, I don't know what to say. I don't even remember falling asleep in the first place."

"Well, at least you woke up when you did, because look way off, over there just between those two clouds." Dante pointed to a large object in the sky.

"Is that...?"

"Yep. There she is. That's Altaria"

Alison's eyes widened. She thought to herself, *"My dreams have been nothing like this."* "I'm seeing a city, an actual city, in the sky!" Alison called out to Dante as she felt a burst of happiness. But it only lasted a second. All of a sudden she became reticent. She closed her lips together and stared off into the distance at Altaria. "What if I'm not welcome...Dante?"

"What are you talking about? Of course you will be welcome," Dante said with assurance.

"Even my own family back home wouldn't accept me. What makes you so sure that your people will?" Alison looked down at her feet. She felt weak again and fought to hold back tears.

"Alison, you have to trust me, my people are not the same as yours."

"I do, I just hope you're right."

Dante then put his arm around her shoulder and Alison could feel the passion in his grip. "Alison you have been a mystery since I met you and since then I have seen a smile across your face, but deep down inside I can feel like I've known you forever."

"That may be so, but I'm nothing great. I may be from

a family of much prestige, but I am nowhere as great as you are." Alison's self-esteem started to diminish as she recalled images of her mother. "And Dante, all I can do is dream about being something instead of actually playing the part. I'm just a dreamer."

"Actually I think that is what's so unique about you. It's like I said earlier, you are special Alison. This is Altaria and here you can have all you've desired." Dante held out his hand for Alison to grab. Alison looked at it and couldn't help but smile.

"You're right," she said, as she placed her hand in his and together they climbed their way down to the deck.

The winds began to strengthen, rocking the ship to and fro. Alison wasn't used to this and she began to feel sick; she wished they were there already. She really needed to get her feet planted on firm ground, and fast. Dante, with a well-balanced stance, stood behind her and placed his hands on her shoulders, steadying her, keeping her safe. The winds calmed as fast as the threatening storm dissipated and soon Allison began to feel less nauseous. But with the quiet breeze doubtful thoughts came racing into her mind again and this time she had a bad feeling about coming to Altaria. Even though Altaria was a beautiful place, even though she was with the greatest person she had ever met, the image of her mother's scorn became overpowering and made her feel as if she was going to collapse.

As they stood on the deck on their approach to Altaria, Alison's hair blew back into Dante's face and the wind carried her scent. "You smell really good," Dante laughed as he breathed in her aroma

"So you enjoy smelling me? Is there anything else I should know you like about me other than my smell?" Alison giggled, relieved because his silly sweet comment helped get rid of the image of her mother.

"So you're Alison, a dreamer who has never sailed on a ship in the sky until now?"

Alison didn't answer, instead she took her hand and pushed him aside and laughed. "So Dante of the skies, am I going to get the grand tour of Altaria?" Alison smirked.

"Well, of course and by yours truly," Dante replied giving her a light push.

"Oh, so you have guts I see. I didn't know you had it in you to push a lady. She laughed as she gave him a push back.

"What can I say?"

"You can start by calling me Queen of the Skies. After all, that's what I am." Alison let loose her smile. She laughed and danced around the ship and held a hand out for Dante to join her. Time went by and as they awaited their arrival to Altaria Alison didn't once think about home. Dante gave her the escape she dreamed of, but why then were the nightmares still haunting her? Alison kept the thought at the back of her mind, but she wasn't prepared to unlock that mystery just yet. She was having too much fun. "So what does the name Altaria mean anyways?" She asked, thinking about how strange it sounded. Dante turned his face to her and whispered in her ear, "Halo."

The morning sun burst the sky into so many magnificent colors, changing and blending with every minute that passed. Alison couldn't help it, but her whole face broke out in a smile of delight as she watched. She was transfixed in wonder and awe. In fact she just about wore herself out from the sheer joy of witnessing this miracle of colors.

"There she is! That's Altaria!" Dante shouted pointing straight ahead.

Alison turned slowly expecting to see a spec in the sky miles away, but when her eyes came to an enormous city floating by itself, she nearly fainted. "Oh, my, it really is amazing, but Dante we are coming in too fast!"

"Don't worry. I've landed this ship longer than you've seen sky ships."

Alison gave him a puzzled look back and thought to herself, *"This is the first and only sky ship I've ever seen or rather been on."* The ship was closing in on the city. Altaria was enormous and from what Alison could see, large stone buildings towered the premises along with what appeared to be statues. Her nerves kicked in and Alison suddenly felt the fear of heights again.

"So what do you think? I told you we would make." Dante's voice surprised Alison from behind.

"Don't scare me like that! Yes, I have to admit you do keep your word."

"Just wait 'till we land. I'll take you all around the city and show you its beauty and just like the stars, Altaria, too, is a wonder."

"You got that right," Alison whispered, still hanging onto the shocking moment of discovery.

"What was that you said?"

"Ooooh nothing... Dante! The ship!"

"What about the ship? He asked.

"If you're here with me, how is the ship steering itself?" Dante and Alison were standing at the front bow and the wind had died down completely, but the ship continued to mysteriously steer under its own control.

"The saphyres at the core is so great in power that it allows its surroundings to levitate, but when pieces of saphyres are near each other, they actually attract each other. In this case the core is pulling us in, but the beauty of it is, its power pulls us in gently and with grace."

Alison's jaw dropped and her eyes widened. Everything was a surprise to her. She thought to herself, *"If this is a dream, I have one crazy imagination."* "I'm ready," Alison finally said with assurance.

"So we're prepared then! Good just you wait. Altaria is only a footstep away and you're about to have your dream come true." Alison's mind stumbled as he said the word "dream." This made a conflict in her head, but once again she focused on her adventure, dream or no dream, she was ready.

With much amazement to Alison, the ship landed gently upon a stone surface of Altaria. They were now in a shelter that to Alison looked like a cave. It was dark, but Alison and Dante could still see, although dimly. The air was thin and warm. In fact, it was the first relief of cold since Dante had held her in the crow's nest. "Alison," Dante said. She turned around and he was back behind the captain's wheel. "My people who tend to the ships will be coming soon. Don't be too alarmed. I don't normally bring guests, but stick with me and I'll take you into the city."

"Good, I'm ready," she replied, but she sensed a trembling in Dante's words. Suddenly she felt a sense of worry in her gut. Finally, just as Dante had said, the people ship's workers arrived. But for some reason it looked like they were running in what seemed like a charge toward The Majesty. Alison gazed all around, ropes flung into the air and onto the ship. Grapples caught hold of the rails and looking over to the side of the ship, Alison saw hands reaching over the rail.

"Alison, come up here with me." Alison didn't take a moment to think. She quickly ran up the steps to Dante.

"Well, well, so you did show up after all, and not

alone I see," the deep voice came from behind the two of them. This made the hairs on Alison's neck stand up. She felt as if a demon had spoken to her. Dante made a dreadful reaction on his face. The element of surprise and stealth had been broken. Dante inside was hoping he could get Alison to Altaria undetected by her. He turned around and looked straight into the eyes of the women who confronted him.

"And it's good to see you, too, Evelyn," Dante's eyes flooded with a slight spark of fury.

Alison felt she was in the middle of something that was destined to get worse. *"Evelyn?"* Alison thought. *"This was the women from before, on that ship we fled from."* Alison was in a state of shock, she couldn't believe that woman was here now, at their very arrival before she and Dante had even stepped a foot on the soil of Altaria. What amazed Alison even more was how beautiful Evelyn was. She almost smirked at the thought, *"Goes to show back home isn't the only place to find pretty witches"* as the image of her mother flowed through her mind. Evelyn wore an emerald green dress similar to the color of saphyres. Her skin was like Dante's, tan, but not too dark, her brown hair was tied back and came down her shoulders and she wore a ring on each finger. She wore a long and dark emerald tunic with armor plates surrounding the fabric. Alison stared at the strange symbol in gold on her chest plate and could feel her dark sense of pride, not just in her appearance, but also her tone.

"You brought a girl from the Earth! You fool! First you flee from Altaria and you return with no honor. But a girl!"

"You don't understand, Evelyn," Dante replied with might.

"Dante, what's going on here?" Alison was frozen to the spot, but her mind was dancing in confusion.

"Alison this...this is Evelyn and she is the queen here."

Alison looked down at her feet and she thought to herself, *"Just when I get the chance to escape my mother and queen, there comes another."* She sighed with the thought, *"This is going to get ugly,"* and Alison, like Dante was not in a state of awe for finally making it to Altaria, but rather in rage for the interference.

"Evelyn, this is Alison. Now I know you're angry, but we can come to a compromise."

Dante's words seemed to have only made the queen even more irrational. She shot a look of evil and despair back at him. "Dante! I'll have you know that this time you're the one who's going to pay. I've had enough of this and now you have really gone deep with infuriating me!"

Alison felt a wave turn her heart upside down. A thought brought her mind to the abyss of complete confusion and frustration. *"Was this all a lie that Dante brought to her? Was Dante just pretending?"* she thought to herself. The way Evelyn was addressing Dante was that he was obviously hiding something about himself and his past.

"Alison, I can explain. She doesn't know me, at least the real me."

"So there is a real you? And who have I met this whole time prior, was that not the real you?" Dante promptly sought the words to say to save the situation from getting any worse, but before he could speak, Evelyn ordered her men to apprehend him along with Alison.

CHAPTER 6

BEYOND A DREAM

"Let me go!" Alison screamed. "Dante do something!"

"I'm the one you want, let her go and take me!" Dante yelled as he fought and nearly strangled himself trying to get free of the guards. They were both placed in iron chains and Alison couldn't believe what was happening.

"You should have listened to the boss, Dante. We have no choice," one of the guards said as one on each side led them through stone corridors that eventually led to a chamber that looked like it was made of rock and other sorts of rubble.

"I'm the one that brought her here, she is not responsible for this. You tell Evelyn to take me and leave her alone."

"Yea, he's the big idiot. I got dragged into this by him and now look who's a victim," Alison shouted with a sense of sarcasm, but at the same time was outraged with Dante and she couldn't hold her satirical behavior any longer. At the same time, her heart sank as day turned into a very, very dark night and the guard's aggressive behavior just added to her fear.

Around the corner one of the guards would light a torch hanging on the wall to purge the darkness. They finally came to a large wooden door where one of the guards took out a brass key and turned the lock to open it. Once open there was another door; this one was iron barred. The guard opened this door and with a swift motion shoved both Alison and Dante into what appeared to be a large cell.

"Wait! I'm telling you, don't do this. Evelyn just needs to hear me out," Dante said in fear. He looked over at Alison, who sat where she fell and kept her head down.

"The queen despises you. You're an embarrassment to our city. This is the best place for you. So this is where you belong," the guard said with a harsh tone. He spat on Dante's shoes as he looked at him in disgust.

"This isn't over! You don't know who you're dealing with," Dante threatened.

"And neither do you," the guard whispered as he closed the final cell door gently. Suddenly the darkness overcame the light and nothing could be seen.

"No, wait, please," Dante could only whisper and was almost speechless. "Alison, help me find a way out of here. It's so dark, but together I'm sure..." Dante paused. His words had echoed throughout the cell, bouncing from wall to wall. "Alison?" he said in a fearful voice. She refused to respond; her faith and hope was deprived and inside she felt broken. This time Dante was the one in more of a state of anxiety, the atmosphere around felt like it had dropped to absolute zero. "Alison where are..."

"Don't try and find me. I can't see you and you can't see me, but that's okay. I don't want to look upon you; you're the reason we're here!" Alison raised her tone and her words echoed along the stone walls of the cell and scorched Dante's ears. He could hear the anger and fear in her voice and this made him feel feeble. Their morale was low, as low as it could ever be, and for a while they sat in silence. Dante wanted to say something, anything, but every time he went to open his mouth, he quickly shut it to avoid making matters worse. He was shocked when after some time went by Alison finally spoke. "You want to know something?"

"By all means, do tell."

"You made me feel happy, happier than I have felt in a long time. For once I believed in love and I felt vigorous. This was the one real dream come true. This adventure, with even someone like you Dante, has been my heart's desire hidden away inside me and it wasn't until that night on The Majesty when you opened my eyes to the real world that I was able to realize that." Dante thought for an instant, *"What does she mean a guy like me?"* "But at the same time, Dante, you have proven all that can be taken away. If I had wanted to be in a place where hopes and dreams could be taken, I would have stayed home." Alison fell silent after her words, and all that she said stung Dante from head to toe. He now felt like the world's greatest disappointment. "That's how my dreams always end and look where we wound up." Dante could hear her grief and feel her heart mourning; it was as though her heart had shattered. The cell became so quiet he could hear the splash of every teardrop that fell from Alison's face. Then she continued, "I'm home, I haven't gone anywhere. I thought you could be my hero to fly me away, but instead you were just an escape for a short while. If I wanted to be thrown into a dungeon like trash, scorned and treated like I needed to be hidden from the rest of the world because I'm not like the rest, then I should have stayed home..."

Dante now felt as if an arrow had pierced his heart. His bones inside shook and everything became cold. "I know, it's funny how you and I are the same. That's why I sought you out and now it's back to reality. It was fun while it lasted though." Dante stumbled in his speech on every word; fear dwelled in his gut and his mind was in utter sadness. If there was such a thing as the abyss of darkness, then the both of them were there. They each felt the bitterness and actually missed the short fun and pleasure while it had lasted on Dante's ship. The dancing, the smiling, the warmth, now all gone. The cell was now an exile to them and they felt so far away from the world.

"Finally some light," Alison thought to herself with a slight bit of relief, *"but where is it coming from?"* The cell had been so dark for hours. With her eyes she searched the whole cell trying to figure out where this light was coming from. Then she realized that night had finally come and the moon glowed through the cracks of the walls. All across this dreadful place, little specs of light flickered like fireflies.

"Alison, I can see you now," Dante finally broke the silence after neither one had spoken a word for hours.

"So what are we gonna do now, any plans?" she said with a serious tone.

Dante just stared at her with a puzzled look as if she had spoken another language. "And what do you mean by plan?"

"You must be joking? You of all people wouldn't have sat this long without coming up with a plan. For angel's sake, I'm ready to get out of here."

"I bet you are," Dante said with a smirk. "But Alison it's not that easy. Evelyn wouldn't have put us in here unless she knew it was escape proof," Dante said with assurance. He actually believed planning escape was pointless. Alison jolted up on her feet and with rapid pace she made her way over to Dante. She stopped only inches from his face and glared into his eyes. Alison grabbed his shoulder and her firm grip gave Dante a shock of her determination, but most importantly he could feel she wasn't willing to give up so easily. She finally let go and took a few steps backwards without taking her eyes off of Dante's.

"Dante doesn't give up and neither do I," Alison said, this time in a much calmer tone and before Dante even had a moment to react or speak a single word, she placed her lips on his. When Alison pulled away the both of them quickly blushed. "Well then, I guess we have an understanding now; we get out of here and it just so happens that I wasn't done sightseeing," Alison said as she laughed with what little happiness that lurked deep within her.

Dante couldn't help but grin as he replied, "You silly princess."

"You know this city better than I do and especially this Evelyn. What does she lack? Can you think of any loopholes?" Alison asked with enthusiasm.

Dante paced in circles letting his mind go off on a ramped journey in the airwaves. *"Plan, Plan, what could we possibly do?"* he thought. Alison walked over to a corner in the cell and picked up a very small coarse stone and waved it at Dante. "Look, this can help," she said as she began in pleasant strokes drawing and outlining on the stone floor as the stone made a chalk residue. She drew a picture of a map, trying to remember all that she had seen as the guards hauled them away into the dungeon. They went up and down many stairs and through several corridors, but Alison's memory was just like her imagination; details could always be magnificently remembered. "Here's where we are," she pointed to an X she marked as their location. Dante looked at her map as if it was no more than a silly drawing a child had drawn with chalk. "We have two options as I see it. If we can get out of this cell we can take the longer journey of sneaking past all the guards and making our way out of the fortress corridors. On the other hand, if only we had some tools and rope, we could get to the outer wall and climb our way down from the wall and escape from there."

Alison was determined and Dante could see that, but he had to break the ice to her. "Alison, you're talking about doing the impossible. I've lived here long enough to know Evelyn has done everything in her power to make this the most fortified place in the skies."

"You're right, she may have, but little does Evelyn know that she has messed with the wrong people. After all I am a strong...we are strong."

Dante now had a grin on his face and looked as if

he was about to burst out with laughter, but instead he nodded. "Right then, let me see that stone you found," he said as if he already had a trick up his sleeve. Dante wound his arm back and with a vigorous force threw the stone through the cell bars and even through the iron window of the first wood door. It clanged and clanged as it skipped across the stone walls and they could hear as the echo let them know the stone had gone a good ways through the dungeon. Dante looked at Alison with that same grin. "Just watch. That will alert the guards and keep them distracted as they go and search where the noise came from which will keep them away from this cell. We don't have much time, just follow my lead."

"You could have told me this plan before making a move," she whispered in a grumpy tone. After the noise from the stone faded away, they could hear the guards rushing and stomping their way down the halls and just as Dante anticipated, their sounds grew further and further away until they couldn't hear them any longer. "You said we have a short window of time, yet we still have two doors to get through."

"I'm already on it Aly. Can you find me another one of those stones like before, only thinner?"

Alison raced to the corner where the other one was, but had a hard time searching the ground through the darkness, so she relied on her hands to feel for stones. "I've got one!" she cheered out loud.

"Shhh, we have to do this with as much stealth as possible." Dante took hold of the stone and reached around the bars of the door to find the keyhole. His hands sought to grasp the key entrance as he remembered; the hole must have been enormous based on the extraordinary size of the key the guard had. "Almost, al-l-most, okay! I've got the stone in the keyhole. Now watch this, a little trick I learned some time ago." Only seconds went by, but to Alison it felt like forever. Dante twisted and turned the stone violently in the keyhole and she could hear his struggle. "If only I could just see it, I can barely reach it to begin with."

"Maybe if you would have told me about this diabolical plan of yours from the beginning I would know how to help," Alison said sarcastically, and immediately regretted her attitude. She saw the sweat dripping from his head and could see the struggle in his face as the bars sank painfully into his chest while he was twisting this way and stretching that way in an attempt to unlock the door. He didn't dare drop the stone. He held on so tightly that his fingers grew numb and his wrist grew so sore that it finally gave out with exhaustion from the effort of trying to reach and twist and turn that stone in the lock, but still it wouldn't open. He finally had to stop and take a deep breath and let his hand rest.

He glanced over at Alison to say something at the same time she took a step toward him and a tiny streak of moonlight coming through the crack bounced a reflection of light from her hair and he whispered excitedly, "Alison, your hair!"

"What about my hair? Is the door budging at all?" she asked.

"That clip in your hair, bring it to me. Maybe we can use it." Alison was astonished.

She had completely forgotten it this whole time. It had a lovely emerald jewel embedded in a setting of small diamonds mounted in gold it and was given to her as part of the royal family jewels. "Alison, we don't have much time," Dante whispered louder. She hesitated for a moment, because this gift had meant so much to her, but her sense of survival and need for escape outweighed the sentiment and she reluctantly handed it over to him. Dante twisted the clip into a thin line and once again reached out over the bars to the keyhole. He gave it a couple of strong and swift turns until finally both of them heard the loud echo of the lock coming undone. To them this was the sweet sound of escape. "Alrighty then, now here we go." He gave the door a good push but it didn't open so easily. "It's just a little jammed, that's all. Come help me push our way out," he said to Alison. She raced to the door and together they leaned in with all their strength, but all they could feel was the door latched back into place. Alison was now hurting from the beating of her own heart as the anxiety had rushed through her blood.

"What can we do?" she cried.

"The only thing we can do. I'm going to reach over with the clip and hold the latch unlocked. Alison, I'm going to need you to shove this door open with all your strength when I say so," Dante now said in a whisper. "Don't hold back. I know we can get through, but I need you to believe."

Alison looked into his eyes almost speechless. She felt like this was her moment to shine, but in reality it was the difference between escaping or remaining in the prison.

"I'll give it my best, but Dante, when I force the door open your hand won't have enough time to get back behind...

Dante put his hand over Alison's mouth before she could finish her words. "Remember," he said, "just believe and I will be fine. Don't worry." He had that glossy charm in his eyes just like the time Alison had seen back home at the citadel. Dante gave her a kiss on the cheek and hurried back over to his position by the door. "Ready?" Dante asked now with fury on his tongue.

"Ready," Alison replied and Dante quickly put the clip back into the keyhole and twisted it.

"Now!" Dante yelled like a roaring lion, no longer caring about stealth or quietness. Alison dashed over to the cell door like a horse in a chariot race and with all her strength ran into the door forcing it open, the door swung back and Alison could hear the shattering noise of what she thought was the hinges of the cell door breaking, but actually was the fracturing sound of Dante's arm. It broke in two places and Dante clutched his arm to his chest and held it in agonizing pain.

"Dante!" Alison screeched and tears immediately flooded her eyes.

"It's okay, I told you I'm strong, I'll be fine. We still have another door to get past."

"Dante you're hurt. Let me take care of it."

"No. Time is up." Dante stood up straight and kicked his right leg forward into the wood entrance door and it came crumbling down. Dante turned to look at Alison who was utterly surprised by what just happened. Dante's face was bright red and a mixture of tears and sweat drenched his body. "If only the first door was as easy as that one, then maybe we would have been out of here a long time ago," Dante said with anticipation and strangely to Alison he smiled at her. She couldn't tell why, but it was with both fury and the desire for escape that motivated his strength and now the true Dante had awakened.

INTO THE DARK

That same field was burning to ash, the flames were high, yet this time Alison was on the other side of the wall of fire, looking upon the scorching remains of what had been a marvelous field. Her flesh stung from the sparks swirling in the wind, but she wasn't afraid and didn't run. She only stood and glared at the fire until its energy faded and the flames were extinguished. Now there was nothing left but mere ash. Smoke rose and circled as the ash still smoldered, but strangely, out of nowhere a chill wind quickly dropped the temperature, catching her off guard and making her shiver. Even the ash cooled within seconds. Another breeze drifted by and this chilled her even more. She finally made a move for safety beside a nearby tree. Remarkably this was the only tree that wasn't burned. It didn't have a sign of scorch on it and was strikingly beautiful. Alison quickly huddled herself against the base of the tree for warmth. She listened closely, but didn't call for help, all she could hear was the sound of her own teeth chattering like tiny icicles breaking in pieces. She looked up at the sky which was just now starting to show off its blue color; the darkness was no longer around. Although Alison was still cold, she believed she was okay for the time being. Up above in the now clear sky, she saw little white flakes falling down to the earth. "Is it really that cold?" she thought, but curiously she was delighted to see snow. "How pretty, but odd," she thought. Within minutes the snow fell faster. Alison just sat under the tree and continued to stare at the falling snow. She even stuck her hand out in the open to catch the little crystal-like flakes. It reminded of her of home when she was a child and used to play in the snow just outside of the citadel making snow angels and throwing snowballs. She also remembered how lonely it was since she was never allowed to play with the other children in the kingdom. Mother never let her around any other children and Alison always felt she was never good at anything. At first she was saddened by this memory, but she didn't sob. In fact, she was actually enjoying the moment of solitude and tranquility, and before she knew it Alison had fallen asleep right at the base of the tree.

The snow continued to fall and caked over her body until eventually her head laid to rest on the snow that collected up around her. Her pale skin seemed to blend her into the snow. She was now freezing cold and her shivering actually woke her up. Alison expected to wake up from this dream, but as she opened her eyes, she lost her breath realizing she was awake and right in the middle of a snow storm. "Dante!!!" she screamed at the top of her lungs, expecting her hero to come save her. But he didn't come. Sounds came in the wind as it wailed and howled like a wolf. "Dante!!!" she yelled again in utter confusion, as if she was stranded on an island at sea. She couldn't scream again; her voice was nearly lost and so was she. "Dante, help me…" she said in the slightest whisper. Those were her last words before falling back in the snow. Suddenly Alison was very startled as something grabbed hold of her ankle pulling her backwards. She desperately pushed and dug the snow away from her feet. It felt like something was crawling underneath her and indeed something was. Wrapped around her ankle almost in a knot was a vine. Slowly it squeezed her leg and a throbbing pain overwhelmed her strength. "Let go!" Alison screamed while rapidly pushing and tugging at the vine to free herself. Alison in rage and fear scrambled to get herself on her feet, but instead, every time she was drug back down to the snow. Still she scrambled to break free, reaching her arms forward grasping the snow piled all around. "Let me go now," she said with a shortness of breath, the exhaustion of lack of energy compelled her down. More vines appeared out of the cover of the snow and grappled her arms and waist. The pressure was now suffocating her and her flesh could feel the agony of the frost. The wind and snow picked up in heavy rhythm and vines slowly pulled Alison toward a nearby decaying tree. Alison, who was out energy and hope gave up on struggling. Her eyes slowly began to close as fate clenched her soul. She wished in that moment that it was all just a dream or that Dante would be there to save her. In the bleak forest realm where she lay she could just barely make out an image of a person coming towards her. Alison could tell it was a man by the way his shoulders were high and muscular and his legs trotted in a determined pace. Just as the man's face became visible, Alison's eyes widened in shock and the world around seemed to become slower than reality. It was Dante! The brisk wind stung her eyes and she quickly closed them and just as quickly opened them again only in hopes of a dream come true. "Whoa whaaat?"

"Stay still and keep quiet and don't make any sudden movements," came the voice next to her as his hand pressed over her mouth. It was Dante holding her close. She could feel the warmth of his body and the pounding of his heart beating against his chest in a state of obvious worry. The room they were in was some kind of cellar, but not like the cell they were once trapped in. It was dark and Alison could only see what was in front of her. "I'm going to take my hand away, but stay quiet. The guards are looking for us." Alison did as she was told but was in a frantic state of confusion. She thought she must have dozed off while they were escaping or maybe she was trapped in another one of her illusions. Dante then looked at her, his eyes gave off a light of emerald. "You fainted on our way out and so I picked you up and tried to make it as far as I could. The guards were ganging up on me and so I stopped in here to hide." Dante whispered to her. The cellar door was slightly opened and the light from the dungeon torch flames glimmered through the crack.

"I thought I was going to be gone for good," Alison said quickly. She was so relieved to come back to reality.

"Say what?" Dante asked.

"Nothing. Just tell me what's the plan, Mr. Genius."

"The guards seem to be circling the perimeter. If we can get behind them we can knock them out and possibly escape through the top like we have planned all along."

Alison smirked after hearing his made up plan and thought to herself, *"Oh, give me a break, you couldn't have possibly been thinking of this the whole time."* Alison was still looking at a different Dante. He was more determined than ever to protect her and get out of danger. Alison placed her hand on Dante's arm, it felt rough and brittle. She then remembered what had happened with the cell door and his arm. "Your arm, it needs to be attended to," she said in a frightened and hesitant tone.

"I'll just have to worry about it later, there's no time." But Alison wouldn't take that for an answer, she held his other arm and signaled for him to sit down. She then tore a piece of fabric off of her dress and used it to wrap Dante's arm. Dante remained very still, Alison could feel his skin turning cold and more tears fell from his face and onto her hand as she bandaged his wound. "I'm okay" Dante said with grim in his voice. He then stood up abruptly and turned to Alison.

"Ready?" He asked in confident tone.

"Not one bit," Alison said softly as she continued to stare at the light burning through the crack of the cellar door.

"Good enough," Dante replied quickly and before Alison knew it Dante had left her side and slipped out the door. "Hurry! Once again time is not on our side." Alison left the cellar as well and stayed to Dante's left side as they jogged up the stone stairs of the fortress.

"Where do we go from here?" Alison asked.

"To be honest, I'm not sure. I actually haven't been inside this part of the fortress since..." Alison looked over at Dante who had a frustrated appearance on his face like he wished he had stayed silent.

"Since when?" she asked hastily.

Dante didn't respond with an answer. "Let's pick up

the pace," and the two of them started to run. Dante had determination on his mind, but for Alison it was curiosity. They finally came to a corner that led up to a small door. They stopped and both become very quiet. Dante looked at Alison and nodded his head and pointed at his ear to indicate for her to listen. They both put their ears to the wood door. This door was different. It had no iron bars across it and fewer bolts. Alison figured this was because it must have been the guard's quarters because they could hear guards talking on the other side. They remained exceedingly silent in order to hear where they may be going to search for them. "I heard about it, but wasn't sure if the news was true. That's why I came to you to see if you've heard anything," one of the guards said.

"Only rumors, but I couldn't believe at the time that they were true," the other guard replied.

"I still can't believe it myself, but they're saying the saphyres and all its force will dissipate soon, it's only a matter of time."

Dante and Alison both looked at each in a mixture of confusion and wonder. "What do they mean?" Alison whispered.

"I don't know, listen closely." Dante pressed his ear harder to the door to achieve better hearing and more vivid images of what they meant by the saphyres "dissipating."

"What is it? I hear nothing," Alison gestured at him.

Dante realized the room on the other side of the door had become silent. "Maybe they left," Alison said in a soft voice.

"No" the remaining of the words Dante was about to say, shattered before they came out as the door rumbled as it opened slightly.

"Wait a second. Remember those two Evelyn had locked up. Don't reveal anything to them. She has them locked up for a reason." The guard said to the other that was about to walk out, but instead pulled the door until it was almost shut. Dante and Alison's hearts were both beating in violent patterns and they both were about to seize the opportunity to hide once again, but Dante wanted to hear more. "Tell me again what plans does she have?"

"With those two pests?"

"No, I mean with the saphyres and all of this kingdom. Surely the great Evelyn has planned to honor her word of protection." The guard speaking looked at the other in earnestness.

"All I can say is stick to the code given to you and don't ask questions. Questions will only get you in a place you don't want to be." Dante, listening from the other side, was now extremely interested in the details he heard, and he thought, *Why did Evelyn truly want us locked away? I understand me, but why Alison? Alison didn't do anything wrong."*

"Dante, let's find another way," she whispered abruptly, but Dante wouldn't budge.

A loud bang came from the room, it sounded like a door that was forced open. They heard people rush in the room. "They've escaped!"

"What do you mean? The boy and the girl? Where have they gone?"

"Get going you two. Search every spec of the kingdom grounds. I want them found!" Alison was now convinced they were close to danger. She grabbed Dante by the arm and the two of them raced back in the direction they came from. The door finally opened and guards poured out with determination to find them. Dante and Alison could hear the running footsteps of the guards behind them. They hadn't been spotted yet, but were out running in the open, not knowing where to go next. They sped around corners leading to other corridors.

"Do you not know this place one bit? Where are we now?" Alison asked intensely.

"Unfortunately, no. This was the one place I tried staying away from." Alison stopped suddenly with her head down low. "Alison we need to keep moving."

"I need to catch my breath. I'm not strong like you, Mr. Fit."

"I'm flattered you think I'm Mr. Fit, but in case you didn't know we have an army behind us.

"What's your next plan, genius?" She asked as she

attempted to catch her breath.

"Right now, the plan is don't get caught. I don't want to leave entirely, we need to find out what the guards were talking about. What's wrong with the saphyres and what does Evelyn really want with us?"

Alison looked into Dante's eyes in disarray. "Back to hiding?" she asked.

Dante looked straight into the iris of Alison's eyes. "Back to hiding…"

THOSE UNSEEN

The footsteps got louder as the guards rushed toward their position. Dante and Alison once again found themselves lost and sought a place for hiding. "Look! There's a small crawlspace in the stone!" Dante said dramatically as he could feel a soft breeze swirl into the corridor.

"Are you crazy? We can't fit through there."

"You're right, we can't, but you can. I've come up with a new plan. I'll distract the guards and you get the heck out of here."

"That's the most absurd thing I've ever heard. We're in this together!" Alison said in panic.

"There's no time. I'll see you on the outside." Dante

led Alison, guiding her to the space and lightly pushing her to get her through. Alison was just small enough to crawl through. "I'll be on the other side waiting for you," Dante said in a pleasant tone and laughed as he said, "It's about time for some fresh air." Alison kept crawling and could see a small light at the end. The crawl space was dirty and smelled like sulfur. Her dress was now stained with dirt and all she could think about was swimming back home in the quiet springs in the kingdom.

Dante now saw the guards approaching and tightened his fists and ignored the pain from his broken arm. He yelled to them, "Let's end this once and for all, no more looking for Dante. He's no longer around. This is your worst enemy." His angry words echoed through the corridor and Dante could feel the rage burning like a fire inside him.

Alison finally reached that light at the end of the tunnel, she was blinded for a moment, but kept crawling. She then realized she had reached a ledge, but it was too late and she fell over. Her instincts reacted quickly as she swiftly seized the ledge and grabbed hold of the stone. "He-e-l-l-p!!" she screamed. Her voice echoed across what appeared to be a valley. It was nighttime and the light in the tunnel had been from the moon above. "Dante! help me!" Alison screamed at the top of her lungs, but then froze as a feeling of deja vu passed through her mind. In that very moment as she held onto the stone ledge, she remembered being in her dream, yelling for Dante in the snow as she had just done. *"Don't look down, don't look down,"* Alison repeated to herself. She didn't have the strength to pull herself up and her arms shook as if they were about to give out. Alison closed her eyes and tried thinking of more pleasant times. She was out of breath and couldn't yell anymore. She opened her eyes and was in absolute awe. The wind was carrying her through the night sky, at least that's what she thought and as she looked behind her, she saw white shimmering wings attached to her back and all around her were angels. They were playing instruments and the melody was so pure it made Alison's ears tingle as if fairies were dancing inside them. Then the angels started to dance as they led Alison safely down to the ground. Still in awe, Alison smiled at the colors that now danced and flashed in the sky beyond the colors of a rainbow. One of the angels approached Alison and held out its hand for Alison to grab and it was saying some words that she couldn't understand. It was as if the angel was speaking another language. Alison tried to grab hold of the angel's hand, but every time she tried, her hand went right through the angel's. "What's happening, what are you saying?" Alison, now baffled, wanted to hear the angel, but more importantly wanted to know what was going on. "Where am I? Take me. I said take me back!" Alison screamed, her perspective now changed and she desired to go back to reality. Her wish then came true.

"Alison, grab my hand," a voice came.

"What? I can't see," she said to the voice.

"That's because you have your eyes closed, silly." Alison opened her eyes and felt pain from having them closed so tightly. Alison grabbed the hand in front of her. It was Dante, he held his good arm out while holding his broken arm to his chest. He pulled her up and she was back on the stone ledge, gasping to catch her breath. "Well, that was a close one!" Dante said to her as he scratched the back of his head.

"You're here, well!" Alison said as she was lost for words. She was about to thank him, but instead replied, "You know you could have gotten here a lot sooner."

"Yeah? Well, you're welcome. We don't have time for this small talk. I know where we need to go, so let's be on our way." With his one good arm he lifted Alison to her feet and they trailed along a stone path that led up in a spiral and went beyond the dungeon.

Dante and Alison approached a ladder that went up a giant stone wall. He signaled for her to start climbing and to not speak in case any guards were around. Dante followed behind her watching out for any guards that might spot them. They climbed and climbed and Alison thought they would never reach the top, but when they finally did she looked down and expected her fear of heights to overcome her. But to her amazement she found by now she was no longer afraid of heights. She had been in danger for so long by now, fear was now just a four letter word with no meaning. They both got to the top and were on the trail that went for miles on top of the city wall. "We're safe for the moment," Dante said. They both crouched down and Dante took a small rock and began to trace a picture on the stone ground with the sharp edge. "From my best memory this is a map of the city of Altaria. We should be here," Dante told her as he pointed. He drew a circle representing the city wall and the homes and towers within the center. "This wall goes for miles and has guards constantly patrolling them, so this isn't the safest place to be, however." Dante paused for a moment, "There's a safe house here and I have some acquaintances I know here," Dante said, as if he knew this was their destination for hiding all along.

"Are you sure this is safe? So far it hasn't seemed like anyone around here is very fond of us."

"I'm positive. There's someone there who owes me a favor anyways," Dante said and nodded at her.

"Well, then, I guess we have no other choice," Alison replied and accepted his plan.

"Right. We need to get to the first tower and the quickest way is to follow this path. Once we get there, we need to find the rope that the guards usually keep in the tower and we can use it to make our way down the wall, which should put us near our destination. Once we reach the safe house, we can hide for the mean time and come up with a plan, or should I say a solution to this mess."

"Let's get going then, Mr. Hero. We won't have the cover of darkness much longer," Alison said eagerly. She was ready for an actual plan instead of these spur of the moment ideas.

Alison's stomach began to rumble, reminding her that she hadn't had food since that morning. As she ran down the path alongside Dante, the hunger pains were now striking her like a shock of lightning and she thought about how Dante's probably just as hungry as she is, but he still showed no weakness. They quickly ran through the cover of darkness to the nearest tower. Alison would constantly gaze over the edge of the wall to see just how high up they were and even dared to imagine the horror of her somehow falling to her death. They approached the tower just as planned, in complete silence. "There's no sense in both of us going up the tower. Two people will cause too much commotion," Dante whispered in her ear. Alison nodded her head in agreement, but then wondered who would be the one to go up the tower.

"I guess it's time for me to show off some courage, I'll go," Alison whispered back in a sturdy voice.

"Are you crazy? Heights don't seem to be your greatest thing. I'll go," Dante said to her.

Alison looked down at Dante's arm which was still

in bad shape and most of the fabric they used as a bandage had torn apart. Alison could see the dried blood that stained his skin and knew she was the only one that could make it up there. "Like I said Dante, I'll go."

Alison noticed the tips of the stone bricks that stuck out from the wall and went ahead to start climbing up the tower. She still didn't dare look down, just kept her eyes on the next step up and the next one and the next one and called back to him, "Catch me if I fall, Mr. Captain of the Skies."

Dante hadn't tried to stop her, but instead he took a few steps back and remained on the path to be her lookout and whispered to her, "Be quiet and don't hurt yourself." Alison knew her only objective was to find something they could use to climb down the city wall. If she could get the rope, they could get off the wall and be on their way. As Dante watched he couldn't help but to think "I wonder what they've done with my ship." He then turned his attention back to the present and noticed her struggle while climbing the tower and feared she would fall. "She is clumsy after all," he thought.

Alison finally reached the ledge of the stone window at the top. It was very high up, but she was able to peek over and spotted a guard with his back turned towards her leaning against the window on the opposite side. She could see a spark ignite from his pipe and the smell of burning tobacco lingered in the drift of the wind. She wanted to grab a hold of her nose as the smell bothered her; she didn't want to start sneezing, but couldn't let go of the window ledge to rub her nose. So she started wiggling her nose instead to stop the sneeze. About this time she looked down for an instant and her heart sank with the thought, "I can't believe we're up this high." Alison wanted to get it over with and any fear her heart disregarded, so she got ready for a quick leap of faith into the tower with the hope there would be an instrument for climbing. She got ready to jump through and counted *"1..2..3"* in her head, but as she got to three and was about to lift herself up, another guard passed right by the window she was now hanging from. She was so startled she kicked the stone wall trying to get balance and keep silent, but pieces and fragments of the stone bricks fell to the ground. Dante at the same time ran for the shadows in a nearby corner.

"What was that? Did you drop something on your way up?" The guard leaning by the opposite window said to the one who just appeared.

"No, it was probably nothing, but speaking of dropping, I got orders from the boss to prepare a drop alright." Alison could actually hear everything that was being said as she was clinging to the wall. She felt like a spider hanging by a thread and felt lucky for escaping a deadly fall for the second time now. She wanted to hear more, but she knew time wasn't on her side. Alison's eyes were flush with the window ledge and she glared right at the guards to see their movements. "Yeah, it's that saphyres you have been hearing rumors about and all the problems with it," one guard said to the other in a stern tone.

"So it is true, and has the plan been developed? I mean they must do something."

"This is straight from the top. Of course, you do know this is a secret and must stay that way. We can't have everyone of Altaria going on a riot spree because of this."

The other nodded in agreement and said, "Any plan is safe with me."

The guard by the window stood firm and looked down at his pocket and drew out a piece of paper that was folded. "All I can say is that the saphyres is indeed in trouble. Take this written order and deliver to the phoenix; if you want more answers you will find them there," he said as he handed him the folded paper.

"I see. Well, I'll be on my way." Alison poked her head all the way over the ledge and lifted herself into a crouched position on the window. Both of the guards had their backs turned towards her and she spotted a coiled rope hanging from the wall. She acted swiftly and moved quicker than she should have. She was now in the tower. She grabbed the rope, which to her amazement was very light, and darted back to the window she just came from. "Well, have a good night. There's been a mess around here lately, things are going to start get interesting," the guard who was leaving replied to the tower guard.

"I'll keep my eyes peeled alright," he said. Alison felt sweat drip from her forehead and onto her lips, she could taste its saltiness and it just made her want to get out of there even more quickly. She tried to feel for the stone with her foot to climb safely down. Her foot slipped trying to find her way down, she caught hold of herself, but the rope shook around her shoulders as she tried to stabilize her position. "Wait a sec it's…it's you!" the tower guard shouted as he looked down the window where the noise came from and darted an angry glare at her. *"Oh no,"* Alison thought as she paused on her way down. She looked up to see him reaching toward her, trying to grab her, as he was yelling, "Stop, Stop! Get back here. What do you think you are doing?" But she kept slowly descending, grasping one hand hold after another, while her feet carefully searched for foot holds.

"Alison, hurry, we've been spotted again, we need to go!" Dante shouted from below.

"Get reinforcements to get these two pests Evelyn locked away. They've been on the run!" The guard yelled down to his fellow soldiers walking the perimeter of the city wall. Suddenly flares that looked like fireworks shot up into the air and illuminated the area where Dante was.

Alison dropped onto the ground of the city wall and ran into the spotlight Dante was in. "Look, I found this, I think it will do. Let's go."

Dante looked at the rope she held in a coil around her left shoulder. "Right, it'll have to do. We no longer get the luxury of a choice." Dante took the rope from her. Working with one hand, he was able to tie it to an unlit torch post nailed to the wall itself. The rest of the rope was thrown over the wall (the side toward the city). "Alright it's done. You go first so at least one of us can get away." Alison knew better than to question the decision; there was no time for it. She felt brave enough to climb just about anything at this point. She had just reached the bottom when she looked up and saw the guards charging for Dante from both sides. He grabbed hold of the rope, threw himself over the side and started his way down as fast as he could. It was hard going down with one arm since he was struggling with the pain. He was now hurting more than before; it even felt as if the blood receded from his arm and numbness set in.

"Come on, come on, I know you can make it," Alison rooted for him. Dante's arms felt like they were on fire, but he found the strength that had built up inside him and before he knew it, he too made it to the soft turf of the outer city. Alison ran over to support him, she threw his arm around her shoulder and after getting him to his feet she looked up for an instant. None of the guards dared to follow them down; instead they stood in a row and watched them get away. The view didn't last long as Alison and Dante did not hang around. Instead they silently slipped into the deep cover of the shadows.

CHAPTER 9

THE HIDING PLACE

The air became thick and cool, which made Alison start to shiver. Her heart was still pounding in her chest from all the excitement that occurred on the city wall. She and Dante had stopped for a moment to catch their breath and Alison took the chance to ask Dante what direction they needed to go. "Look, that sure looks familiar alright," Dante said in a cheerful tone. Alison turned to look, following his gaze, but all she could see were small lights in the distance, that reminded her of the fireflies back home. "Now that sure is familiar," Dante said while gazing at the dancing lights.

"What's familiar? All I see is something glowing in the distance."

"There," he pointed, "street lights, Alison. Come on, I'll show you," Dante encouraged her as he grabbed her hand. Then they cautiously walked towards the lights. Alison and Dante still knew to stay out of sight and keep their eyes peeled. As they approached the street lights the color of the flame turned from orange to a light blue.

"Did you see that Dante? The…the color of the flame changed!" Alison exclaimed.

"Actually the color of the flames didn't change; that's just your eyes deceiving you. In fact the flames have always been blue." Alison was very puzzled after hearing this and didn't know what to say or think. "I bet you would even be more surprised if I told you that those flames inside the streetlight lanterns are actually saphyres." For once Alison wasn't the least bit surprised. This journey of hers had been full of so many surprise that nothing was new anymore. "Saphyres is a mineral though, how can it be in flames?" Alison asked.

"Well, that's the beauty of it, isn't it? You see, saphyres may be a mineral that we harvest, but the one that you experienced before, which powered my ship, gives off enormous amounts of energy. This energy can be obtained in different ways and over several years we have learned many ways to capture that energy and have been able to use it in different forms." This was quite interesting to Alison and it made her think why saphyres was only found in the city of Altaria and not back home. "Wanna see a trick of mine?" Dante asked Alison with a sly grin on his face.

"Well, whatever floats your boat, Hero, if you must," Alison replied sarcastically. "Actually saphyres does float my boat, thank you very much, and what you're about to see involves this saphyres." Dante replied and then quickly reached for the streetlight, pulled it off the post and lowered it to the ground. Alison could now see the brick pavement they had been walking on and she turned her head left and right looking at the little homes nearby. She could see beautiful stained glass windows with the night dew dripping down the seams. This place was like no other Alison had seen before. There were large towers far in the distance and one of them had an enormous clock like the one in the town back home. Each home was made of stone that had a sparkle in it as if pieces of diamond were growing out of it. She even noticed an alley between a few of the homes exposing what appeared to be a stream or river flowing through the town and a stone bridge linking to another side of the city. This place even reminded Alison of a dream she had once. "You done daydreaming yet?" Dante said to her.

"I don't know what you're talking about. I just can't believe..."

"Believe what?" Dante asked as he opened the small door of the lantern and reached for the flame. Alison gasped and was about to yell, "Wait, you're going to burn yourself!" but before she could get the words out something flying through the air just barely missed her face and she could feel the streak of wind blow her hair and dress. The object struck the glass of the lantern and broke it. The flame grew high in the air and made Dante step back for cover. They watched as the flame grew and grew and in a flash it disappeared. Dante saw that a pebble was shot towards them. "Wait! Stop! It's me!" Dante yelled up at the rooftop behind Alison. She couldn't see who he was yelling to but knew they must have been spotted and all she could think about was how tired she was from the last runaway they were on and neither one of them had had much rest. The moment became silent as Dante stood there with a stern gaze at the rooftop. No more pebbles were shot and Alison slowly turned around to face their foe. She could see a shadowed figure slide down the roof and jump off the ledge and drop smoothly to the ground in a crouched position. Alison could now see the person as he was under the street light. He wore a tunic similar to Dante's and had a hood covering most of his face. Alison could tell it was a man by his broad shoulders and muscle, but he was shorter than Dante. He was standing there still and firm as a rock and as Alison was so focused on waiting for him to reveal his true identity she didn't notice the sling he had pulled back and was aiming directly at them. Dante stepped in front of Alison without a single hint of fear in his eyes. "Jas, it's me!" Dante yelled as stepped further into the light.

The hooded man quickly lowered his sling and unveiled his hood. His hair was brown and almost as long as Alison's. He had a very noticeable scar that ran down the cheek near his left eye. Alison tried not to stare, but was quite curious what he had been through to get that. "Dante my goodness, what are you doing here? Don't you know everyone is looking for you?" he asked.

"We're quite aware of the situation, Jas," Dante replied and then turned to Alison. "Jasper, this is Alison. She's new in town and I've pledged to keep her safe. Now can you get us into hiding for a short while? There's much to discuss."

"Are you crazy? They're going to realize the both of us are gone and then what?" Jasper replied abruptly.

"Both? Jasper what have you gotten into since I've been gone?"

"Evelyn's put me on a special task group. A lot's changed since you left and well...now responsibility has definitely taken its toll on me," Jasper said with the desire for Dante to see how much he'd grown in the ranks.

"Doesn't matter, just like the old days. You know we've never pledged our allegiance to Evelyn and besides you still owe me for the crater incid..."

"Okay! I get it, no need to repeat that day!" Jasper said quickly with grief. Alison could see that same grin like before sweep across Dante's face.

"Good, then we have an understanding."

"Come, you and your friend need to follow me. These streets aren't safe at the moment." Alison then grabbed hold of Dante's arm and pulled him to face her.

"So back to hiding?" she asked eagerly.

"For now yes, but if you liked my ship just wait till you see the nest," Dante said in a proud tone.

"The nest? What are you guys, part bird now?"

Dante smiled to her question. "Something like that, Come on. Jas, go ahead, lead the way," Dante said and grabbed Alison's hand and they both ran alongside Jasper. They made very sharp turns as they followed Jasper, running through the night along the brick roads. Finally Jasper stopped so they could all catch their breath.

"Wait, Dante," he whispered. "You and Alison get back into that shadowed corner. I hear people coming this way." Jasper pointed over to a corner in a small alley between two homes; it was unbelievably dark in there.

"Alison, let's do as he says," Dante said to her. So the two of them stealthily crept to the dark corner, pulling themselves as far back into the deepest shadows as possible.

"Who goes there!" a deep voice of a man came.

"It's Jasper. Stand down. I've got this area under control," Jasper replied to the voice. He could see the guards approaching, each with a sword on his side and holding torches in their hands. "Well, well, what do we have here? They might as well be looking for you as well as the others," the guard said with arrogance.

"Well, Zar, I didn't expect to find you here either. Like I said, everything on this side of the city is fine," Jasper replied.

"Don't make me laugh, you little pipsqueak. Where are they? You know as well as I do exactly who Evelyn wants. You better hand over your friend to me," he yelled to Jasper, but Jasper showed no signs of guilt or weakness.

"I don't know what you're talking about. Dante was a fellow comrade of Evelyn and nothing more. I have no need to hide anything," Jasper responded just to toy with him.

"Don't mock me! I know the friendship between you and the other pipsqueak is very strong indeed and the first sign of any connection between you and them escaping, I'll have you both appear before the boss, dead or alive. That I can promise."

Jasper inhaled a big breath of air as if Zar's words were starting to get to him. "No, it's like I said, I want to capture them as much, if not more than the likes of you, and when I do don't think for a minute I won't outrank you by the graciousness of you know who."

Zar spat at the ground near Jasper's feet as if Jasper's words had delivered the final blow. "We'll see about that," Zar said and turned with his group of soldiers and trotted off into the shadows of the city. A few moments passed by before Jasper turned to face the corner where Alison and Dante were hiding and whistled at them. The two of them came out into the open.

"Coast clear?" Dante whispered before crossing to the other side of the street.

"As far as I'm concerned, but we don't need any more close calls. You know how cunning Zar is," Jasper said and Dante nodded in acknowledgement. Dante and Alison crept over to Jasper and they all sat in the shadows of the nearest alley to catch their breath and come up with a strategy. "Well, there's only one way around this mess. There are guards everywhere, but one place, or should I say places, and Dante you know what I'm talking about," Jasper said as he stared at Dante and knew he knew exactly what was being implied.

"Oh, geez, well you're right about one thing, and we sure are tired from running," Dante responded and looked at Alison with that same look of guilt she had seen before.

He went to open his mouth to explain to her what they were thinking, but before he got the words out she remarked, "We're going on the run again aren't we? And here I was thinking we were far enough away that we could rest for a change." Dante recognized her angry change of tone.

"If we stay here we will surely be captured and if we flee then we will have at least a half a chance of getting away."

"Half a chance!" Alison said in frustration. "And tell me...how exactly are we going to get out of here hopefully undetected?" Alison was confused and eager at the same time.

"The rooftops," Jasper responded to her.

"You mean...?"

Dante and Jasper, both with a stern look on their faces, gazed at Alison and then looked at each other as if they were becoming allies for the first time. They then both said simultaneously, "Rooftops."

CHAPTER 10

THE HOLLOW TREE

Alison struggled with the scorching heat pounding on her. The day was exceptionally bright and there wasn't a cloud in the sky. She was in a corn field running for her life, but couldn't remember which direction the enemy was coming from, and that wasn't the worst part. She had been scratched up by constantly running through the corn stalks and occasionally tripping over roots growing out of the ground. Her energy was low, but she couldn't help but run. She even yelled to herself *"Stop!"* but couldn't. The paranoia set in and took its toll on her mind; she just knew she was being followed. Alison called out for help like before. "Dante! Where are you!" The atmosphere was silent, but hostility still sat in Alison's mind, and moments later an echo of the very words Alison yelled came out of nowhere. "Dante! where are you!" The echo sent a chill up her spine as she knew that wasn't her voice after all. She paced all around, looking in all directions like the stranded little girl she was. "No, no, where's the way out of this maze?! It has to be somewhere around here," she exclaimed dramatically out loud. Even by now Alison still could not recognize or put together the pieces of the danger she was in and why she was there.

All of a sudden she could see the silhouette behind her, a silhouette of something a lot bigger than she was. She feared to turn around to face the danger, but she slowly turned around anyway, taking heavy breaths as she was afraid, yet curious. The sun beamed down on her and its rays made it hard for her to decipher exactly what was in front of her. She placed her hand up to her forehead to shade her eyes to see. It was an enormous figure in front of her and although Alison thought it had approached her, maybe she had approached it instead. A small cloud out of nowhere drifted in the blue sky above and rested in place blocking most of the sun. "A tree?" Alison said out loud. "I've never seen anything like it, but how could I have not seen it before?" Alison was now in deep thought as her mind paced to decide if she was in fact still in danger. "Hello! Is anyone out there!" Alison yelled in the direction of the tree. It was an enormous oak. Its roots grew above ground going several feet in all different directions. The branches were long and thin and full of leaves that carried small green crystals that sparkled like little spots of light. *"That looks so familiar. Where have I seen that before?"* Alison wondered.

An immense breeze blew suddenly and some of the leaves fell off and were carried by the wind. One in particular drifted down towards Alison's hand. "Saph... Saphyres?" Alison said in a soft tone. She caught the leaf holding the mysterious crystals and examined it more closely. "It's saphyres! I knew..." Before she could finish her words, the ground shook and became more and more violent to the point Alison could hardly stand. She knelt on the ground and gazed up at the tree which was now stripped of all its leaves. The bark started to rot and the roots dried up and broke apart. Alison remained kneeling on the ground; with her hand she grasped some of the gravel beneath her as she held on trying to steady herself.

Moments went by and the savage wind settled down into a soft breeze. Alison, still gripping the earth, was exhausted. It was as if the wind stole every ounce of energy from her body and scattered it all around. She looked up and noticed the tree was now completely dead. In fact she could tell it was now hollow inside by the sunlight passing through the cracks of the bark. "But how? Where do I..." Alison exclaimed aloud and then paused to think of a direction to go to leave this mess behind her.

As she got up from the ground her legs wobbled; they were still without stable energy. She licked her lips and realized just how dry her mouth had become. She also noticed the little leaves carrying the crystals of saphyres that fell were no longer around. The corn stalks were still all around and she wondered if they somehow had miraculously grown a few more feet because she now couldn't see far in the distance like she had been able to before.

She started to turn slowly in a circle trying to cover everything in sight all around. "Dante where are you! I'm ready to leave now!..back to Altaria." Her voice became faint and then she panicked as she realized she suddenly couldn't speak any more. "Mmmm!" Alison started to mumbled frantically. She even tried using her hands to pry her mouth open to speak. Her movements became weak, so much so that she collapsed to the ground.

Alison finally wore herself out again and just spread her arms and legs out like a mangled body. She was frightened, but at the same time she just wanted to close her eyes and dream. As she tried to close them, memories of the past came swarming into her mind. She thought about the snowy winters that used to occur every year back home and how she would escape the citadel for a short while to lie in the snow and make snow angels. She then started to move her arms and legs around in the gravel as if she were back home in the snow. Alison remembered the stories she used to read in her father's library when she was younger and how she would play around the outer citadel pretending to be the characters she read about. It was pure joy filling Alison's heart, but then a flood came as the lonely memories poured in. She saw how desolate her life was. She never had many friends and even her family scorned her.

Alison knew deep down she wanted to cry, but the sea of memories she was in revoked it, the flood had already drifted her out to sea. For what she thought would be one last faint cry for help, she softly muttered "Dante..." Her senses came back to reality. Alison was still lying there on the ground looking up at the highest branch of the hollow tree. Her eyes felt as if they had anchors on them trying to sink to the bottom of the ocean. As they slowly closed again she caught a glance of the top branch falling from its peak straight toward her. She knew she was done, but by now felt somewhat relieved and accepted whatever may come.

The branch dropped down toward Alison and in the midst of the moment a voice came, a quite familiar one to Alison. "They're gaining on us come on!" All Alison could see was complete darkness, until she felt a strong tug on her wrist. "Alison, Jump!" Suddenly that darkness was gone and she found herself leaping through the air from one rooftop to the next alongside Dante. Jasper was up ahead a few feet and as Alison came back to herself she took a moment to figure out what was going on and where she had been this whole time.

"Dante why are we running on the rooftops and who from? We're going to cause too much commotion."

"I've been trying to get your attention forever since we left the alley. You keep dazing out like you're a ghost."

"Is that so?" she responded. Alison was still emotionally affected from what had happened with the tree and all the memories that besieged her.

"Yeah. You were going off on some kind of little adventure," Dante replied as they continued to hop from one rooftop to the next. Alison suddenly became speechless. It was as if Dante knew exactly where she had been with the hollow tree. They were now on the other side of the stream that flowed through the city. They finally were headed to the heart of Altaria, which was both a good thing and bad. "The center of Altaria is where the safe house is. Bad news though...that's the most guarded place of the city," Dante said. Alison couldn't believe that was where he was taking her.

"So your so-called safe place happens to be in the center of Altaria? How convenient!" Alison yelled with sarcasm.

Dante didn't respond. Instead he looked back and noticed even more guards down below on the streets following their movements on the rooftops. "Let's pick up the pace and show them what we're made of Jas!" Dante shouted toward Jasper.

"We're almost there, just a little further. I think I can see the tree from here," Jasper called back to Dante and Alison who were one rooftop away from him. The word "tree" caught Alison's attention and she started to feel quite weak as the words crept up her spine as if that branch that had been falling off the hollow tree finally landed on her.

"Dante, where exactly are we going? I need to know now!" Alison demanded as she slowed her pace to get the words out.

"Look, there's no time; just trust me," Dante replied. He now noticed Jasper had disappeared. "Well, he could have waited for us before going down. I guess that's Jasper for yuh," Dante mumbled to himself.

"Wherever we are going we need to get out of view." Then she stopped as if mesmerized by the glory of what she saw. "Look, the sun is rising," she whispered as she pointed toward the eastern sky where the sun and all its golden burning rays were just starting to peek over the horizon.

"I see," Dante responded as if he were out of more words to say. "Over there is our destination, hurry let's go! We're going to drop and I must warn you the first time doing this can be a little..."

"A little what?" Alison asked frantically.

"Okay, stop right there!" A deep voice came from Alison's left side. She and Dante came to a halt and looked to their left only to find four guards pointing their swords at them. "Well, well. Look what we have here, a little girl and an exile. Now you're done for good." Dante and Alison remained speechless as they saw even more guards had climbed up to the rooftop and now nearly surrounded them.

"Plan genius?" she whispered to Dante who stayed silent, but his usual the *"I have an idea"* grin swept across his face.

"Well, Zar. I'm surprised it took you this long to find us. We made it over half way across Altaria without you hooligans spotting us, slacking are we?" Dante said trying to taunt every nerve in the guard's body and laughed as he wanted it to upset him.

"We will see who's laughing after we take you back before the boss," Zar grinned back. Dante grabbed Alison by her arm and gave it a slight squeeze and slowly stepped to the edge of the rooftop giving a shudder as he looked over the side.

"Look, all I'm saying is, if you really wanna get around a city like this, all you have to do is...Jump!" Dante yelled and leaped off the edge while pulling Alison down with him.

"Dante!!!" She screamed all the way down. They landed inside a funnel-like object that took them into a tunnel and they slid fast careening first to the right and then to the left and then straight down. "Where are we!!" Alison screamed again.

"Hahaha, Dante laughed. I wanted to tell you about this before, but didn't get the chance. Just hold on!" The tunnel was dark and they were now moving at a greater speed. Suddenly they could start to see a bit of light at what she hoped was the end of this insane travel.

"Sir, what now!" one of the guards exclaimed.

"After them you fools!" Zar demanded, but like before none were willing to dive off the rooftop after them. "You -- take some to the west wall, and you -- take a team to the grounds of the city to find where they will surface, they'll be coming up somewhere." Zar commanded the guards.

Alison and Dante were racing to the light, the metal slide was slick and there was almost no friction to stop them. "Hang on tight one more time, the ride's not over just yet," Dante called encouragement to her.

"Give me a break, not over?" she hollered back, her voice echoed throughout the tunnel and then all of a sudden they were out in the open air. They fell down through the air and for a moment Alison forgot about the fact she was falling downward and thought she was back in the corn field when she caught a glimpse of that same old, hollow tree. "The tree," she whispered softly to herself in midair. Suddenly something grabbed hold of her arm. It was Dante. She snapped out of her daydream and closed her eyes when she thought they were headed straight for the ground.

"It's okay. We'll be okay," Dante's voice came through and gave her ears a warm feeling as if the words promised security. She couldn't reply as the serenity that set in her was so comfortable she felt like she could die with a smile and no regret. There was a black hole-looking shape below; at least that's all Alison could see. As soon as she accepted the moment of death they both landed on what felt like a giant pillow. It sent a shock of surprise through Alison's body as she felt both relieved and confused.

"Whoa, what's going on? What did we just hit? Dante, where are you?!"

"Geez, you got any more questions?" Dante teased as he tried to swipe dust off his pants.

"It's mighty dusty in here," she complained as she coughed hard. Alison noticed her voice didn't echo and it was once again completely dark and cold just like back in the cell. This made her concerns rise and she began to wonder what kind of safe place this could possibly be.

"Don't worry. I can make some light," Dante said. He took a stone out of his pocket, the one he had kept from the stone cell. Then he grabbed hold of something Alison couldn't make out, but saw a spark as he swiped the stone against what he was holding onto. "There we go," he said as a small candle in what appeared to be a lantern was now lit. "Stay here. I'll get some more light going." Alison stayed put and watched as Dante circled the room, lighting each of the lanterns on the walls. Confusion sank in as Alison couldn't figure out where they were. The walls were a dark brown and had all kinds of creases and small cracks running in all directions. The place was now completely lit. Alison turned back around and noticed what they had landed on was some kind of big pillow. It was marvelous. The pillow reminded her of home with its beautiful purple stripes and gold buttons that bordered the trim. She was astonished with the entire place and she was in complete awe when Dante walked over to one of the walls and pulled back a curtain and moon light burst through the night illuminating the safe house.

Although iron bars blocked much of the outside from the window, it was still quite fascinating. She couldn't believe they had been traveling for so long. It was already dark. "Night already? You gotta be kidding me," she said shockingly as she thought about the gorgeous sunrise they had seen not long ago.

"Remember now, time does go by faster up here in Altaria. It's just how it is," Dante reminded her.

She then turned to face him. "This is some kind of safe house, huh?" she exclaimed as she couldn't stop gazing around the place. There was a winding staircase that led several stories up. There was a long table made of wood with four chairs on each side. "It almost looks like..." Alison paused before finishing.

"Un huh, go on. I think you have an idea what we're in." A chill ran up Alison's spine along with the words *"it can't be"* flashing in her mind. She was curious after all, but knew why it looked somewhat familiar. "Our safe house...where we stand as we speak...Believe it or not, we're in one big tree, the biggest in all of Altaria. It's hollow all the way to the roots and for me this is what I call home," Dante said with a serious and frightening tone. He then burst out into laughter. "Ha! I can't imagine what you're possibly thinking right now. I'm sure you're shocked from seeing first a flying ship, a floating city and now a big tree!" Dante said still laughing, but Alison wasn't laughing. She kept her head down low and stood still in the moonlight.

"Do you really expect me to believe we are where you say we are?" Alison knew her question was vague and not necessary. It gave her chills as visions came so rapidly through her head she couldn't even make out the images.

"That's right, Aly. Welcome to the safest and most hidden place around...welcome to the hollow tree."

NOTHING LIKE HOME

Alison could feel the presence of someone else in the hollow tree. She turned and saw Jasper as he walked into the main room out of one of the dark corners. "Jas, there you are," Dante said. He now spoke with more seriousness in his voice.

"Well, the coast is clear. I checked the streets just outside and found out most of them looking for us are held up just past the town square. Evelyn's guards must have thought we made it that far. I guess in this case it's a good thing they are overestimating us," Jasper said proudly.

Alison sat down on the big pillow they landed on earlier; her legs were tired and her feet were sore. She then took off her royal shoes, which by now didn't look very royal, and laid back making herself right at home. She still couldn't believe they were actually on the inside of a giant hollow tree. "And you both call this place safe? This tree must be huge. How can no one know about this place let alone see an enormous tree growing around the heart of Altaria," Alison exclaimed. Dante and Jasper both looked at each other and then turned to look at Alison who still felt vulnerable to reality. By now she couldn't tell what was real and what wasn't. Her mind raced like a chariot of horses.

"Look…you rest for now," Dante said to Alison. This time she didn't refuse, she slowly closed her eyes and tried her best to feel relaxed.

"Dante, I promised to get you this far, but you can't hide here forever. Why have you brought her to Altaria with you?" Jasper said quietly so Alison wouldn't hear him.

"Let's head up top, we'll talk more there," Dante replied. So the two of them climbed the spiral staircase up past a few floors. They reached the last floor which had a hatch that could be opened in the ceiling. They climbed through it and were now on the outside standing on one of the hollow tree's large branches. "Jas, you know I didn't want it to happen like this. After I left Altaria I went to visit the Earth down below. Alison doesn't know this so keep quiet…The winds were rough one night and I noticed my ship's saphyres wasn't working like it's supposed to. This made me very suspicious, so I tied the ship up near some kind of fortress on the Earth and went to look for shelter, along with food and water. However, I found this girl and well...I brought her with me," Dante said.

"But why? You know that was foolish," Jasper replied sharply.

"Because I didn't want to cause any commotion...And besides that, I didn't think she would actually agree to leave home to come with some stranger." Dante defended his actions and was determined to show that it wasn't a mistake.

"You know Evelyn pretty much wants your head. When she told you to leave the first time and you fled she didn't expect you to actually come back and not to mention to bring an Earth girl with you."

Dante stayed quiet after hearing Jasper's words. He looked out into the night sky and felt the life of Altaria flow in the wind. "What about you and the rest? Everything is so different now," Dante asked.

"You know I didn't have much of a choice...me and the others became imperial guards after the clan broke up. Yes, our lives are different now, but you know it was for the best, Dante. We couldn't keep scrounging around for food on the streets and barely making it. Evelyn actually gave me, as well as the others, hope and a role here." Dante turned his eyes to Jasper and now gave his full attention. "Look, I know it's not what you want to hear, but you need to. I'm sure we can work something out...you and that girl can't be on the run forever," Jasper said with his hand placed on Dante's shoulder.

"You said the others joined Evelyn's force as well?" Dante asked.

"That's right and don't think for a minute that we don't have your back...to a certain point that is," Jasper replied.

Dante now looked straight into his eyes with intent. "I need to know something and we can be on our way. I know I'm putting you in danger by being here."

"Ask away, Dante, but don't worry about danger. You know as well as I do Evelyn doesn't know about the tree," Jasper replied.

"The saphyres core," Dante said slowly making sure he really caught Jasper's attention.

"What about it? We're still mining as usual," Jasper answered.

"Don't play stupid with me Jas," Dante said, and Jas quickly turned away as he held guilt inside.

Jas gazed at the white lights of the city glowing in the distance. "So you have heard? Well, I know very little myself. What do you want to know?"

"I want to know how the saphyres of Altaria could be in danger. We've been mining and harnessing its power for generations. What could possibly be going wrong?" Dante asked with a wave of vigilance in his voice.

"All I can tell you is that Altaria doesn't have much time. I do know Evelyn is aware that the saphyres core is losing its power drastically."

"Well, what changes have you seen? Everything seems normal now!" Dante exclaimed.

"That's because you haven't seen the core..." Jasper responded. "No one has seen the core, it's impossible to get even close to the core, you know that! I do know...I know that what you also haven't seen is down below," Jasper said as he looked down at his feet.

"Down below?" Dante questioned, confused.

"Look, as we both know Altaria mines from the bottom up and lower Altaria...it's been falling apart, crumbling if you will."

"Do they know how to stop it?" Dante asked, but rephrased his question. "Do we know how to stop it Jas?"

"Evelyn and the ones really close to her have been working on it and keeping everyone else in the dark. Strange times are coming Dante and I don't have a good feeling about it. Evelyn has been strengthening the walls and guarding every square inch of Altaria. I'm suspecting she thinks it's some kind of plot or treason."

"Treason...treason for what? How could someone possibly be responsible for something like this and what would they want to happen to Altaria!?"

"To bring it down Dante...to bring it down," Jasper said, and Dante became silent again as he tried to process the plot.

"The night sure is getting chilly, Jas," Dante told him in a muffled tone.

"Slightly," Jasper responded. Dante crossed his arms to keep warm. "Maybe you should check on the girl," Jasper proposed.

"Her name's Alison," Dante replied.

"Awe... Alison, that's her name...well then, goodnight to you my friend." Jasper said and started to walk away.

"One last thing Jas...where are the rest?" Dante asked sharply.

"Oh, they're around...a lot closer than you would think," Jasper replied and walked through the door and was in the tree and out of sight.

"Well, that's interesting...very peculiar," Dante whispered to himself and decided to go back into the hollow tree himself. He slowly climbed down the winding stairs and walked over to where Alison had fallen asleep on the entrance pillow. He crept over to her side quietly as he didn't want to wake her. "What?" he asked as he heard her say something. She said it again and this time could make out what she was saying "Where's home?" she said softly and by her motions Dante knew she was dreaming.

Alison was now back home, but peculiarly was

standing in the middle of a great storm at nightfall on one of the outer walls of the citadel. Lightning struck all around, but disappeared every time before reaching Alison. Even the drops of rain themselves disappeared completely before landing on her head. She felt a rumble beneath her feet as if an earthquake was starting. Suddenly black crows came out of the clouds and swarmed the skies. They followed in a circle as they flew above Alison. She quickly raced to get off the wall and into the citadel, but stopped all of a sudden when she realized there was a huge gap in the wall and swung her arms backwards trying to catch her balance. Then she turned to run in the opposite direction; thankfully there was no gap this time and she just knew she would be home free. As she came close to the tower the storm became more violent and she had to leap for safety as the wall came crumbling down, breaking into small pieces of rock. She swiftly grabbed hold of one of the last stone ledges remaining and there she dangled, fearing for her life as slowly her fingers started to slip onc by one. With hope losing its place in her heart, as finally the last finger slipped from the ledge, her eyes widened with fear as speechlessly she plummeted toward the earth. "Alison!" she heard a voice come from the sky above. "Alison, wake up and snap out of it!"

"It's over!" Alison yelled as she woke up and found Dante next to her shaking her arm.

"Yes, it's over, take a deep breath," Dante said as he comforted her. Alison now couldn't remember what had just happened or why she even yelled "It's over." Dante handed her a small flask of water and held it up to her mouth. "It's over okay, now drink up; it will make you feel better." Alison took the flask and drank. Drops ran down her dress as she was still uneasy and couldn't stay calm. "You must be famished. Look, I managed to scavenge around for some food…it's not much, but it will satisfy your appetite for now," Dante said as he held out a piece of bread. He split the bread in unequal pieces and gave Alison the bigger half. She took it as if he held gold in front of her. "The sun should be coming up soon," Dante said. Alison's mind reflected back to the sunrise from earlier on the rooftop and how marvelous the colors of the sky were. "Now then, we will stay here for a few more hours and then I'd like to get to the bottom of this saphyres…I just have some unfinished business to do. Will you join me?" he asked as he opened a small box next to him and took out a pocket watch to check the time. Alison paused as she was about to respond, but didn't. She was baffled by the mysterious watch he had pulled out and quite strangely it looked like an exact replica of the one her father used to have. She still remembered him taking it out of his pocket to keep up with time as they used to walk through the fields outside of the kingdom.

"How did you get that?" she asked hastily.

"What? This old thing, it was a gift," Dante replied. His voice then lowered to a whispered. "A gift from long ago."

"It's beautiful and it reminds me..." Alison paused.

"Reminds you of what?" Dante asked.

"My father had a pocket watch just like that once. I used to see it every day when I was with him. After he was gone I never saw the watch again," Alison said. A slight frown formed across her face, as talking about her father always brought her down. She could no longer cry over him as if she had no more tears left to shed. His memory slowly faded over the years, but still rested deep down in her soul; it was still a part of her.

"Alison what happened? He was a great man wasn't he?" Dante asked her.

"Yes, he was, the greatest person I ever knew and if only everyone in this world were like him, it wouldn't be so dark and shallow all the time."

"Tell me about him," he asked as he came closer to her. They both sat with one of the small lanterns lit between them and Dante listened to her story of her father.

"My father was known throughout the whole kingdom, and I mean by everyone. He grew up as an orphan who lived on the streets and begged for food and water just to stay alive. I also know that all the towns in our kingdom faced scarcity of food and many other resources our people had once thrived upon. When my dad was a child the ruler of the kingdom was greedy and loved power, so much that he took advantage of everyone around. I don't remember much, but I overheard that my father was actually a direct bloodline of the royal family. I don't even know how they came to this discovery, but what I do know is that the king became ill and my father was crowned at the throne as just a boy the very day the greedy king died. Supposedly there was a prophecy, but even that was lost long ago before I was born into the world."

Dante was amazed by her story, it was thrilling and mysterious. "So he ruled for quite some time, huh? What did he do for the land?"

"He brought peace, Dante…" Alison said and paused for a moment. "Peace and prosperity…no longer did people suffer from the heart of a greedy ruler, but instead found a light that glowed in my father's heart that was filled with generosity. He grew the kingdom in spite of the people being practically on their knees begging for life and he gave them hope of a better future. The poor were no longer unsatisfied and the council of the courts cheered his heart of charity," she told Dante. He said nothing as he listened closely to her words. "It was all great, Dante…until one day he was gone and the hope he gave to our people was deprived once again."

"He left?" Dante asked, but felt he might have asked too much.

"One day a great storm came and mother told me to stay inside because it wasn't safe. My father was notified of the dam leaking at the northern gate and it wouldn't hold much longer as the flood continued. He chose to go to the dam with the rest of the men to stop it from wiping out the villages. I watched it all from my window. I saw my father and the others ride on horseback to stop the flood. I watched as they laid one sandbag on top of another in order to save the dam. He had volunteered to be the one to climb to the top of the dam to place the last bag of sand to stop the water from seeping in. As he did the stone beneath his feet cracked even more and crumbled down to the flood bringing him with it. The waves were violent as the kingdom was near the sea. I was told he tried to swim and fought the waves, but moments later he was carried away and was never seen again," Alison told him. She now found the tears she held back earlier and the atmosphere of the hollow tree became desolate. Dante then placed his arm around her. "My family was destroyed forever and so was the rest of the kingdom. Someone so kind and careful was taken away just like that." Dante didn't respond at first, he just continued to comfort her.

"So that bedroom window of yours…that was the one you looked out of to watch him help save your people."

"That's right," she said.

"How brave of him…how brave," Dante said in a

whisper.

"What about you."

"What about me?"

"You never told me your story, why you left Altaria and what your life has been like here and for angel's sake, how did you come across a hollow tree to live in?" Alison asked with curiosity.

Dante turned his face away from her and searched for a place to begin. "Well, like your father, I, too, am an orphan. I never knew who my parents were and I was raised by the elders of Altaria. Evelyn was chosen by the elders to one day lead when we were both young," Dante told her, but Alison was already confused as she knew Dante and Evelyn weren't on good terms yet they had grown up together.

"So you and Evelyn grew up knowing each other?" she asked.

"That's right. She, too, was raised by the elders, but she was always seen as the best and was treated like a spoiled little princess, always getting what she wanted," Dante exclaimed. It reminded Alison of her mother and how her own mother neglected to treat her with any tenderness. "After Evelyn became a leader of Altaria she was given authority of leadership over the guardians of Altaria, or in other words, the guards who protect Altaria. I was asked to join many times, but refused. I went down a different route than Evelyn. I chose to leave the palace of the elders and live my own life my way. I was looked down upon, Alison...still am. I, too, was tired of home and that's why I left," Dante said in a stern tone.

"But that's not really why you left. You didn't have a choice did you?" Alison said firmly.

"No...you're right. I was told to leave. I had made a remark to the leaders of Altaria, including Evelyn. I said what I really thought of this place and they challenged me to live away from here; in other words I was exiled."

"But why would you speak against your home?"

"I just wanted to discover more out of this life. Up here everything always goes one way," Dante said. But Alison didn't understand what he had meant by "everything was one way."

"So why Earth and why me, Dante? Did you think I really needed to change?" Alison's words struck Dante more than she realized and started to regret the way she made it sound.

"I just wanted something different for a change. I felt unwanted here, as if I ever just disappeared no one would realize I was gone. That's why I didn't argue against those who challenged me to live on my own outside Altaria."

"So you're just like me...huh?" Alison whispered with a melancholy tone.

"What was that?" Dante asked.

"Oh...nothing, just thinking maybe you can make things better this time." Alison told him.

"Yeah...just maybe," Dante replied. The two of them sat quietly for a moment as the gloom soaked in from the two of them realizing feelings that hadn't been let out for some time. "Alison, I want to show you something," Dante said as he reached his hand out for hers. She took his hand without questioning what he wanted her to see. He took her up the winding stairs and through the top hatch out to the large branch where he and Jasper had spoken the night before. The day was now coming to an end as Alison could feel night approaching. The sun was setting smoothly on the horizon and gave just enough light that she could see almost the entire city from where they were. "Just a few more moments and you'll see," Dante said, but Alison didn't understand. She couldn't believe that they had actually been in the hollow tree for a few days. It seemed as if time was in a race that Alison herself couldn't keep up with. The sun finally disappeared and darkness of the night came and brought along hundreds of stars with it. "I remembered how great you thought this was back on the ship," he told her.

"Dante, it's beautiful, even more beautiful than before!" she exclaimed. She stood next to Dante and slowly leaned her head upon his shoulder. Together they both gazed up at the stars of the night sky and were once again in awe of how dazzling the world really is. "By the way, Dante," Alison said, "you never told me how you got your ship."

"Ha! You're right. I didn't mention how I got that old thing," Dante said. But he remained silent and didn't tell her where it came from. He just looked back up at the stars and knew it didn't matter because that night the only thing that was setting sail was love.

Chapter 12

SAPHYRES

"Well, there's your sunshine again!" Dante said cheerily as he woke Alison up.

"Already? Geez, you people don't get any sleep around here, do you?" she replied while wiping her eyes.

"You just gotta get use to it, that's all."

"This constant time change and being inside a tree is really getting to me," Alison complained.

Dante just grinned and waved for her to come over to him by the window. "Come look," he said. Alison went over to the window and peeked out. In the distance she could see the town square and people walking about amongst the city. It was the first time she had really seen the many people of Altaria. "You wanted to show me a crowd of people?" she asked.

"That...that is how we are going to get around!" Dante exclaimed, but Alison was too tired to figure out what he was getting at. "I thought about it last night and I came to the conclusion that the only way to stay undetected by Evelyn is too change our outfits. We need to look like them, just ordinary folks."

"And how is that going to happen? We always seem to bring a lot of attention to ourselves," Alison said.

"With these, Alison," came Jasper's voice. He appeared out of nowhere and startled her. She also noticed it was the first time Jasper acknowledged her by her name. He was holding extra clothes in his hands and showed them to her. "I brought these for the two of you and notified the others; they should be coming along soon..." Jasper paused as the hollow tree shook and a great vibration came from the surrounding walls. Alison was nervous and didn't know what was going on. "Well, speaking of them..." Jasper said as suddenly two people flew out of the slide and onto the pillow below. Then another came, and then another.

"Well, well. What do we have here? Look what the cat dragged in," came a deep voice. The swarm of people who came in gathered around Alison and Dante. They were a mixture of men and women who were wearing similar outfits as the guards, only theirs were more colorful and appealing. Alison was slightly shy and found comfort in standing next to Dante. "So the family is all here now, I was wondering if you all would show up."

"Oh, we've always been around. I've followed the two of you for three days now. Why do you think the coast was clear half the time? I had to call my men off your trail to help you escape. I hope you didn't think you were just that clever, Dante," a young women spoke up from the group. She was quite short and wore a hood over her head which covered her face, but strands of her dark red hair showed. Her skin was pale like Alison's and she wore a gold chain that bordered the hood over her head.

"I had a feeling all along we had eyes on our backs, Marcy," Dante replied. The girl kept her head down low and Dante had a look on his face like he had been betrayed. A smile finally appeared. "Well, what a relief, so you guys kept a close watch on us, huh?" Dante said. A person in the back of the group stepped forward. He was a strange-looking one and Alison had to hold back her breath as she wanted to laugh. The person was extremely skinny with tight evergreen pants and wore a chest plate with a symbol of a feather on it. His face was hidden as well. He wore a bizarre studded helmet that had a mask like a knight with a nose piece that stuck out like a plague doctor. He threw a bag onto the floor in front of Dante. It was opened and inside Dante could see there were normal civilian clothes. "Disguises. So you're right, Jas. They've been very close. Just doing some shopping around the bazaar, I see," Dante implied.

Marcy then removed her hood. "That's right and The Apothecary here...well it was his idea," Marcy said. The bird-looking knight just stood still as a statue not saying a word. Alison didn't anticipate Marcy being so beautiful. Her eyes were crystal blue and her cheeks carried a rose color to them.

Another member stepped forward and stood in front of Dante and gave him a slight bow. He then turned to Alison and did the same. He then grabbed her hand and laid a kiss upon it. Alison froze and started to blush. "It truly is a pleasure my friend and, Dante, who might this be?" the man asked. He was charming like Dante and had long hair, almost as long as Alison's and had pointy ears like an elf.

"Well, Laboo, this is Alison...from Earth," Dante replied. Laboo froze, as he couldn't believe what he just heard.

"An Earthling? You've done it this time haven't you? Can't get much worse for you can it, Dante?"

"You never know, Laboo, but while you're all here..." Dante stopped short as Marcy interrupted.

"Speaking of us here, we can't stay long. We've got to get back to duty soon."

"You all have really become Evelyn's right hand men since I've been gone, huh? How can you all live with yourselves?" Dante exclaimed and the room became silent.

"Like I said, Dante, things have changed. We've all moved on. In fact this is the first time all of us have been back to the hollow tree in a long time. Alison was surprised to hear this. *"They talked as if they had lived for ages yet they all look so young,"* she thought. "At least tell me about the saphyres," Dante demanded. Each of the group members looked at each other as if no one wanted to be the first one to say anything.

"Altaria is losing altitude in the skies. We know the core is losing power rapidly, but we don't know why and we can't get any more about it from the elders," Laboo told them.

"What about the people? Since I heard about this mess, I haven't seen anyone around the city panic about this. How can that be?"

"I'm not even sure if Evelyn herself knows much. None of us do," Marcy said to Dante. The Apothecary stepped forward next to Marcy and motioned his hands on his armored chest plate as if he were doing some kind of sign language. "The Apothecary is right...none have been to the center where the core lies and besides, mining has been shut down for days now," Marcy exclaimed.

Suddenly in the midst of their talk the hollow tree started to shake and the ground below them, too. "What's going on!" Alison cried out.

"I don't know, it's coming from below us!" Dante

yelled back. Each of them held on to something in the tree. After several moments the shaking stopped and they noticed that cracks had formed in the walls of the hollow tree.

"That has been happening, too, lately," Jasper said, who was behind Dante sitting on the floor.

"I need to speak with Evelyn," Dante said. "She's got to know more than she's willing to talk about, but I've got to convince her to say something."

"Are you mad? Dante we're wanted by her. You're practically a fugitive!" Alison told him.

"Dante, I'm not so sure she knows more and your friend is right. We all can scrounge up whatever we can, but as far as this is concerned we never had this meeting and we never spoke with the two of you," Laboo said as he knew it was dangerous for any of them to be even speaking with Dante and Alison who were wanted.

"I'll find a way into Evelyn's chamber. There I will find what I can and somehow make amends. Then I'm going after the saphyres," Dante declared.

"You're crazy," Alison said to Dante, but turned to the others and said, "But after all, he's right. We can't just sit here hoping for this place to be saved. Dante is onto something. I know you all don't know me well as we have just met, but over the last few days Dante has not only showed me trust, but I owe him my life as he has saved it countless times and I'm sure he has done the same for you all as you are his friends as well. Help us, I beg you. This is the greatest place I've ever been to and this beautiful kingdom you call home needs hope," Alison said. She couldn't believe the courageous words she had spoken. She felt as if a spirit inside of her gave her some wisdom. Dante too was shocked. Never had he seen Alison like this before and he thought, *"She's not so little, after all."* Dante smiled, but the rest of the group just stood, not in awe, but still with the same look that things like that are only great and said in fairy tales.

"Jas, you best be getting back as well," Laboo said to Jasper.

"Yeah, I know," Jasper replied. He got up and walked over to where the group was standing, but stopped short and placed his hand on Dante's shoulder. "Good luck, pal. You know we still have your back, just not your ideas... sometimes," Jasper told him in a mellow tone.

"Yeah...thanks...a lot."

Jasper gave him a wink and walked over to stand with the group. "We will be around, Dante. Remember we are never too far and...take care of Alison." Laboo said. They each took a few steps back. Marcy walked over to the nearest lantern on the wall and blew out the flame. The area where they were standing became dark. Dante took out his stone again and lit the lantern that was just blown out. Once again that part of the tree was lit, but they were all gone.

"Well, that's impressive," Alison said with an angered voice. Dante remained quiet as he looked around, trying to think of a quick plan. "Speaking of this, how did they get out of here. I mean how are we going to get out of here?" she asked frantically.

"Oh, there's a way," Dante assured her. He walked over to where the group had been standing before. "Come here and I'll show you. It's about time for us to leave this old place anyways," he said.

Alison walked over to Dante, who remained still and calm. She wondered what he was up to as far as getting out and back into the city. She looked down and just below their feet was a square space in the floor. "Oh, give me a break not agai...nnn!" Alison yelled as they went through the floor and back down a metal tunnel. They slid slower this time and straight with very few turns. Alison could see this time, as sunlight shined through tiny holes in the tunnel. They slowed down greatly and stopped just before their feet touched a small door that looked like a vault.

"It's still going to be a little dark before we reach the city," Dante told her.

Alison wanted to be relieved of this excitement and really needed to get some fresh air. But fresh air is not what she got. "What's that smell!" Alison asked while holding her nose. Dante had opened the door and as they stepped inside it felt to Alison like they were underground.

"That...that is the smell of the city sewer my little Earth friend," Dante replied with a laugh.

"We went from being inside a giant tree to being in a sewer? You gotta be kidding me."

"Don't worry. I'm taking you to the way out and into the city square. Look, don't draw any attention to us and once again just follow my lead," Dante told her. She had no objection; she trusted him and was looking forward to finally being outside. "Grab hold of this and climb up and out quickly." Dante led her up a ladder and opened up what turned out to be the sewer lid. They both poked their heads out into the open and were relieved at the fresh air flowing into their lungs and the ray of sun gathering in the pores of their skin. "Alright, let's go," he said and they both climbed out. They were behind some bushes and shrubs, just a few feet from the brick pavement of the city. "I managed to grab these from the group before they left," Dante said and showed her a pair of clothes. They were men's clothes; one had overall straps and was used by the mine workers and the other was a worn pair of brown pants with a grey wool jacket with a white undershirt. Dante showed Alison the wool jacket and pants. ". . . and this one would be yours."

"Mine? If you think I'm getting into something like that then you're out of your mind!" she replied. She looked down at her own dress she wore and after seeing how dirty and torn it had become it wasn't much better than the pants and coat.

He also handed her a cap to wear. "Take this, too. This will hide your long hair."

"So you want me to look like a boy?" she replied sharply.

"Just until we get into Evelyn's chambers and then we can book it out of there and save Altaria."

"So you really are determined, huh? The boy who left his home is the one who will be saving it after all," she said sarcastically. The two of them went behind separate trees and changed quickly into the other clothes. Alison now looked very different and made Dante laugh.

"Well, now, and who might you be, sir?" Dante said, laughing.

Alison took her hand and playfully hit him on the head. "Yeah, more of a man than you are," she replied.

"Alright, settle down, let's get a move on." Dante held her hand and they both walked amongst the people in the city square. The streets were heavily populated as the townspeople went about their day shopping through the markets. Alison saw butchers hanging meat out to sell and elderly ladies weaving and spinning cotton and others sewing materials into clothing. "Just stay by me," Dante whispered to her.

"Where is her home? Is it where we were back with the ship?" she asked.

"No, but close. It's up there...just look," he told her and pointed up an enormous grassy hill that had a narrow path of stone that led up to what appeared to be a palace at the top.

"So you all have a place for the royals just like back home huh?"

"Actually no. No one is royal. That up there is the court of the elders and there Evelyn has a chamber of her own. Let's just say she doesn't get out much." The crowd started to get thicker as they walked further into the heart of the city. Buildings were stacked on top of each other several stories high and there were so many structures and homes Alison couldn't keep up with what was what. They finally came up to a solid black wall that stretched around the perimeter where the hill started.

"And how are we going to get around this?" Alison asked.

"Maybe not around, but definitely under," Dante replied without facing her. "Come on, this way." Dante and Alison rushed to the right where a short stone bridge led into an alley.

"We're not going back into town are we?"

"No, not at all. Evelyn is definitely up on that hill. I feel we're running out of time, so in this case were taking a short cut," he said. They carefully walked down a slope to the left of the bridge until they were now completely under it. "Jasper once told me about this passage. The guardians once used it as an escape in case of hard times."

"Oh, great, here we go again," Alison replied to him.

The tunnel had a candle on the wall which Dante grabbed and used it to light their way through. As they got closer and closer to the court of the elders the passage became more narrow and the materials of the wall changed from a rocky grey stone to a smooth green stone. It reminded Alison of the color of saphyres. They suddenly came to a stop when they reached a tight crawl space. "I think we can both fit through but only one of us is going to be able to see what's ahead. I'll go in front and you follow close to me. There's got to be a shaft somewhere through here. Since this was once used as a secret escape, there's no telling where we will end up in the court, but we need to reach her chamber soon," he said, and they crawled their way through, this time without a light. They moved several feet ahead and soon they could hear voices within the court. As they crept closer they could recognize what was being said but not who the people were; Dante didn't recognize a single voice. Just a little further ahead there was a small ray of light beaming through the shaft they were in. It was coming from an open space within the floor, allowing light from down below to breach in. Alison couldn't see, but Dante stopped and peaked his head over slightly to see what the commotion was. Alison knew to be quiet as a mouse since the voices came from right below them.

"And the core." "What about the core?!" "We're taunting ourselves over this by doing nothing!" "What can we do?" "Do you really expect us to know how to actually travel to the core?" "It's impossible, I say!" the men shouted down below. Dante could now see them seated around a giant table and to Dante's surprise they were all the elders of Altaria. Dante didn't expect them to have been on this side of the court. He remembered as a young boy playing throughout the court and that the elders didn't use this side of the palace court to have council. He recognized quite a few of them and remained still to eavesdrop.

"I know one who has an idea." A voice came from behind the table, but it was too far for Dante to see who it was. "There is one here who has come closest to the core among you all, closer than anyone." Dante then recognized who it was. "Evelyn," he whispered to himself. Evelyn walked in a circle around the table where the elders were seated. She pointed to an elder who was seated on the far right. "This man! Lazarus I have now learned you were there when Altaria was founded and were amongst the first of our kind to acquire saphyres!" she hollered. The court wasn't too surprised as they had known only one amongst them was a founder of Altaria.

"Madam this makes no difference. Lazarus has aged like the rest of us. He is now nearly blind and he sure can't make it to the core," an elder told her and the others rambled on in agreement.

"I will go you fools! Just lead me to the right mine; my most loyal men will venture with me," Evelyn said.

The room suddenly became quiet as each of the elders looked at each other in despair. "Madam we don't know which mine, in fact none of us know if there is a mine that leads to the core," an elder replied to her.

"Altaria sits in the hands of utter collapsing. Is there not one of you who is brave enough to come forward with knowledge of this core?" Evelyn yelled in anger. The elders were now furious at her demands and they got up from the table one by one and walked to the entrance of the chamber.

"We're done here," one of the elders said to Evelyn as they passed by her and went out of the chamber.

Evelyn stood there with her arms at her side and gazed at the floor, her pride stood in the way of her feeling defeated. This time she no longer looked like an official of the city, but a leader ready to defend its walls. She wore magnificent armor that was the same color of saphyres and even had an emblem on the chest plate that represented a saphyres stone. Dante slowly and stealthily crossed over to the other side of the shaft. He signaled for Alison to cross carefully. She was nervous and desperate to keep calm. She had begun to sweat and panicked as she heard a creaking noise that came from the walls of the shaft. It felt as if the walls were starting to tear down.

She reached her hand for Dante's, but looked down at Evelyn who was still standing in the chamber below. A drip of sweat fell off Alison's face and she knew it was all over for them. "Oh, no," she whispered. The drop fell directly onto Evelyn's head who then looked up and spotted them.

"It's you!" she yelled up at the shaft when at the same time the shaft started to shake and crumble apart.

"Alison, jump!" Dante yelled to her. They both held each other's hand, interlocking their fingers together and jumped simultaneously. They landed straight on the table below. Dante quickly got to his feet, but Alison laid flat on the table, groaning and holding her left arm which was in pain from the fall.

"Dante!" Evelyn screamed at him.

"Look, I know what you're thinking, but hear me out, please. You wouldn't believe what we've been through in the last few days...well maybe you would since you have had everyone chasing us, but please, I can explain," Dante said, trying to get all the words he possibly could get out to save them from the embarrassment.

"I'll have you know you're not getting away this time Dante, surrender yourself now!" Evelyn drew out a sword that she kept in a sheath on her back.

"Well, it's been awhile since we've done this, just like the good old days when we were kids, isn't that right, Evelyn?" Dante said trying to upset her. She charged at him, but Dante quickly jumped onto the table and then onto the other side. "You stay put, this shouldn't take long," he told Alison, who was still lying on the table. "I know about the saphyres, Evelyn. I can help, but I need you to trust me."

Evelyn smiled and began to laugh. "Ha! You really believe you can reach the core? No one has ever done so, you fool."

"But I do know one thing, Altaria is hollow at the center and I know our best chance lies near the bottom of Altaria. I've been told the further toward the bottom of this floating rock, the easier it is to dig further to the core," he told her and she reluctantly lowered her weapon.

"I guess fighting you really isn't worth it as you're still clumsy and foolish as ever. Yes, it's true that Altaria is more brittle toward the bottom, but climbing down that far hasn't been done since Altaria was first discovered."

"I see, and let me guess, no one has dared to try and make their way down that far? I'm also willing to bet some of the old mines are still down there along with the structures and tools for digging," Dante said to her. He could tell she still thought his words were a waste of time.

But instead, she replied, "And if you're thinking of using an airship, it won't work, the winds below Altaria will send you flying around like a bird with its head cut off. And furthermore, I can't imagine you would be stupid enough to try and rope your way down that far."

Dante thought for a moment and thought how he could accomplish the task. "Maybe climbing isn't such a bad idea. I do happen to be one of the best climbers in Altaria," Dante pointed out.

"Yeah? Just like that time at the giants bolder and..."

Dante then interrupted, "Okay, okay! No need to talk about that again." He looked over at Alison, who was getting up from the table. "You're okay, right?"

"Definitely. I've had much worse happen on this adventure."

"Good. I think it's time for us to be on our way. Evelyn, tell me what you can and I just might be able to save Altaria," he said and suddenly the chamber started to shake again violently. It tossed Dante to the floor, Evelyn held onto a lantern on the wall and Alison took shelter under the table. Finally it stopped and Dante got to his feet.

"Alright, I'll support your little plan, but I can't expect you to come back."

"Good. That's all I need, Evelyn," he said sincerely.

"I can only tell you one thing that you don't already know and that is some of the elders as well as myself have been aware for some time about a continuous growth of poisonous roots discovered throughout Altaria. We never thought it would cause any harm up until recently, when we have found what could be a link between that and the saphyres losing its energy," she told him. Dante was curious by what she said and wondered just what they may really be up against. "Go…Now," Evelyn said to Dante and Alison. The two of them just stood there gazing into Evelyn's eyes which were filled rage. "I said go! But when I see you again…we have some unfinished business to take care of.

Dante looked back at Alison who was looking down and holding her bruised arm. He motioned for her to follow him and they both ran side by side out the entrance door. They found themselves at the top of a large set of stairs and quickly ran down and through the last door. They were now outside in front of the elder's court looking down the grassy hill that led to the black gate. "Let's go find that core. We've got everything on the line and no time to spare," Dante told Alison. She looked into his eyes and he looked back into hers and never had he seen so much courage in the eyes of a friend. She nodded in acknowledgement and together they made their way down the hill. Evelyn was standing on the steps leading up to the court watching Dante and Alison as they chased hope. She shook her head and whispered, "Make it back, Dante…make it back."

THE ROOTS OF ALTARIA

"Where do we even begin?" Alison asked. She was still baffled with the plan and the direction to go. *"What did they mean by the bottom of Altaria? They can't actually be talking about the bottom of this floating kingdom, can they?"* she thought to herself as she and Dante made their way back through the town square attempting to stay undetected and reach the border of Altaria. Alison thought about the way they were headed and started to think, *"Maybe this isn't the best idea."* She stopped suddenly when they reached one of the back alleys going between two market stores. "Wait. Aren't we just going straight toward the wall…where there happens to be hundreds of guards roaming the path?"

"Actually this way won't take us toward the wall. I didn't tell you before. I guess I figured it wasn't too important, but the wall doesn't actually circle all around Altaria. Indeed there are some spots where there is no wall, and I happen to know one." Alison didn't respond; she had learned to trust his judgment and even admired his commitment to protect his home, the very one he was asked to leave, thinking *"and now he's come back."* "We've got a ways to go, but we need to reach the other side by sundown," he said. Alison didn't reply, she held her arm against her chest and still felt the throbbing from the pain. "Stop." Dante suddenly motioned for her to get against the wall of the long alley they were in. "Guards are coming," he whispered.

She whispered back, "I don't understand. Evelyn knows what we're going up against. Why doesn't she just call off her guards so we can save Altaria?"

"You know she won't do that. Evelyn is going to protect her pride no matter what. It's how she's always been." Bad luck had really settled in as they both realized there was no easy escape in the alley they were in, only forward or back. "I guess we're both up for climbing I suppose," and Alison laughed at his pun. It seemed the adventure no longer scared Alison, but no matter what direction Dante went, she was happy to follow. "Here, grab hold of this. Hurry, they're getting closer." Dante guided her hands to a metal pole that ran down a wall on the side of the market. It had hooks attached to the brick allowing her to hoist herself up to the top.

Suddenly a guard spotted them and called out, "Stop them!" and the rest of the guards charged at them trying to block their escape.

"We have no choice. It's going to be another pursuit on the rooftops. Hurry!" Alison was able to scramble to the top with Dante right behind when one of the guards caught up and grabbed hold of his foot. He began kicking and squirming and yelling, "Let me go you idiot. We don't have time for this."

But the guard held tight, trying to pull Dante back down to the ground. "You pesky brat. You're the one everyone has been looking for and I bet there's a good price on your head." The guard had a tight grip on Dante's foot and suddenly he felt his shoe starting to slip off, even to the point that he was able to use his other foot to finish pushing it off.

About that time Alison had reached the top and was reaching back down, yelling, "Grab my hand!" and she pulled him up to the rooftop alongside her.

He looked back over the edge only to see that the guard had fallen down with nothing in hand but Dante's shoe. "Well, that's the most you're going to get from me," Dante taunted sarcastically as he made fun of the guard, which of course made the guard angrier than ever.

"Get the rest of the search party and go after them,"

the guard yelled to the other ones.

That's all it took for Dante to grab Alison's hand and they took off running, crossing from rooftop to rooftop. Even in the midst of this fright, she noticed the sun setting back down on the horizon and paused to admire its beauty. "Hurry," Dante urged here. "We don't have time for that luxury now. We need to get to the core somehow. Come on." Just as they leaped to a rooftop a few feet below another shake came from the grounds below. This by far was the most violent one they had experienced. Dante pulled her to make her lie down on the surface of the rooftop, waiting for the shaking to let up, holding onto each other in fear. When it settled down a bit Alison looked just over the ledge and saw the people in the streets running in all directions seeking shelter, fearing for their lives. Mothers held their children close as they screamed while others panicked as they searched for their loved ones. "I know it doesn't feel like it, but this is the perfect time to get away. Let's go," Dante urged and tried lifting her to her feet.

"Are you crazy? I can barely stand!" she cried out, trying to stay balanced as the ground continued to rumble and shake.

"Come on. I'll help you." Dante grabbed Alison by the hand and they leaped to yet another rooftop. This rooftop was quite long, and looking beyond it Alison didn't see anywhere else to jump to. They ran as fast they could as the rooftop started to crack all the way down; it seemed as if the crack was chasing them. "Once again, when I say jump...well, jump!" he hollered as they fled for their lives. They both came to the edge of the rooftop, but Dante had no intention of stopping there. "Jump now!" Dante yelled as a booming noise came from behind them. Just as they jumped off, the rooftop collapsed and all its brick and stone crumbled to the ground. They were in mid air and in that moment Alison couldn't wait for a safe landing...until she looked down and saw nothing but sky below her. They had jumped off the edge of Altaria. "Alison! Reach!" Dante screamed as he tried desperately to grab her hand. He managed to grab hold of an odd-looking guardrail and as Alison fell through the air he grabbed her hand to save her from the fall. But the hold of hands didn't last, his palms were sweaty and he barely hung onto the rail himself. Alison's hand slipped out of his and she was now falling toward the Earth. "Aliso-o-on!"

The moment became still to Alison as she watched the sun in the distance fade like dying embers. It reminded her of the view from her window back home. She could feel that familiar breeze that caressed her face and touched her softly like an angel's hand. In that moment she thought about the kingdom grounds that stood strong and still like a mountain and the birds dancing among the clouds as they circled her home. It was the first time in what seemed like forever that she actually missed home and surprised herself to death when she actually realized she missed her family and that's when tears fell down her face.

THE RISE, THE FALL, THE LOVE

Alison woke up to the sound of a nearby spring splashing as if a child were swimming. The air was very warm and there was no breeze blowing. She noticed the pasture she was lying in was barren except for glowing embers. It was as if a great fire had come in and scorched the field. In fact everything around, including the trees were just as scorched. Everything except the beautiful spring was destroyed. Alison was curious and got up to dip her fingers in the fresh water of the spring. She looked down into it and was delighted with the crystals that bounced in the waves of the water like fairies dancing. But something wasn't right. She expected to see her face; she figured by now her face would be dirty and worn from her adventure, but she saw no reflection. *"No reflection?"* she asked herself. She looked all around to find out where she was. The only memory she had before waking up was being next to Dante on his ship The Majesty. The sky started to turn grey as if a storm was starting to form. She saw small glows of light all around the sky that twinkled like stars. Standing next to the spring, her body lost balance and the sense to care and she fell gracefully into the cool water. Her whole body felt like a feather falling from the clouds. She was now under water sinking slowly, but she had no nerve in her to do something about it. She closed her eyes and let the water take her down as bubbles formed all around. *"Wait! What am I doing here? I can't die...this can't be the end."* She knew being under water there was no way to breath, but something in her motivated her to take a breath and to her amazement she was actually breathing underwater. She floated all the way down till her feet were touching the sandy bottom. A rumble in the ground then began as if an earthquake had just started. Suddenly an enormous creature dove into the spring and presented itself before Alison. *"A dragon? It can't be...this isn't real!"* she yelled in her mind.

The dragon before her bowed its head. *"Ahh, but I am real."* The dragon spoke to her without opening its mouth to say a single word. Alison could hear the dragon in her mind speaking to her.

"*Where am I? I no longer feel in danger, but why?*" she asked him without a single bit a fear lurking in her heart.

"*That is because you're not in danger little one. Come, I will show you the heart of courage beyond your dreams,*" he told her and turned his back toward her. The dragon was crimson red and swayed like a snake. It had no arms or legs, but could move around in all directions. Its fangs were sharper than a blade and its whiskers were long and black.

"*Could he really mean for me to climb onto his back?*" she thought to herself.

"Yes, come, let me show you. Destiny awaits."

"But how can you hear me? I can speak to you in my head?" she asked.

"*There are many things that can be done, and I will show you both the light of the stars and the darkness of the shadows.*" She was utterly confused with his words, although she chose to trust him and climbed onto his back. "*Hold on little one; we are going beyond what you know,*" he said and Alison was about to speak when she lost her breath of words as the dragon, with her clinging to his back surged up out of the spring, straight upward, soaring through the sky. Somehow Alison was now wearing a dress that she remembered as a gift from her father. To her amazement she was not soaked from the spring; not a single drop of water stained her dress. She and the dragon soared toward the sky and in that moment

Alison felt like a free spirit. They were now gliding above the clouds. Alison closed her eyes to absorb the moment and when she opened them, she noticed that the sun had died down and the night had come. The stars swiveled all around like comets searching for home. The dragon continued to soar higher and higher and its body swirled like a serpent.

"*Where are you taking me?*" she asked the dragon.

"*I will show you what will come in time, and time is the journey that never ends,*" he responded as his body swirled more violently, gaining speed.

Alison felt a spark of heat seize the flesh on her neck as if hot wax from a candle slowly dripped on it. She saw the night sky as it started to brighten and knew something wasn't right. The stars one by one plummeted past her towards the land. Great orbs of fire raced toward the spring and the nearby fields. The falling stars came right for the dragon and Alison. He increased his speed and made sharp turns as he dodged the stars. "I've seen this before, it's happening again. This can't be destiny!" Alison yelled. This time her mouth actually opened as she spoke to the dragon.

"*This isn't the end, little one. It's only the beginning,*" the dragon once again responded as a voice in her head. She looked up just in time to see a piece of a falling star directly above her head, falling straight toward them. This time the dragon did not turn; the fragment hit the dragon on its back. Alison tried desperately to hold on as the dragon had become weakened and Alison too felt she had lost her strength. "*Stay true to your dreams Alison. They make you who you are. Yours will forever come true,*" the dragon said in a faint voice as his eyes slowly closed and then he turned into a dive back toward the land. Alison didn't want to let go, but the dragon burned quickly into tiny embers and was no more. She could only say "*goodbye*" as she, too, fell toward the spring that was now shallow and in ruins.

Alison felt a warm tingle in her arms and felt like she was no longer falling. She closed her eyes for a moment and when she opened them she was looking directly at the sunset. The sight was so beautiful, the orange rays burst in the sky like a wave of fire. She then saw the sky around and realized she was in mid air, but not falling; rather she was being taken upward slowly. As she looked to her right, to her amazement she saw what Altaria looked like from underneath. Suddenly her attention turned to her chest where she felt a warm feeling that took a dive of joy to her heart. Then she noticed a glow of green light beaming from her coat. Alison now felt a sensation of strength and serenity. She didn't try to resist, she was in awe at the beauty of Altaria from a different viewpoint. As she drifted upward she heard a voice call to her.

"Alison, I'm here!" It was Dante who called as he

waved his hand to her in utter joy. He was on small stone ledge that connected to the side of Altaria. It had a black iron rail that led across it. Alison started to float toward him, her back was toward the Earth below and she kept her eyes on him without saying a word. "I've almost got you, just a little closer," he urged as he put his hand out to reach hers. "Alison, you're okay!" Dante exclaimed with relief as he pulled her down to the soft turf on the ledge. The stone was covered in grass, weeds and vines that were growing through the cracks and draped over the edge.

"Dante where are we?" Alison whispered.

"We made it...we actually made it," he told her in awe. "What's that glowing inside your coat?..it looks like..." Dante said and Alison sat up quickly as she too wondered why her coat was glowing. She undid one of the buttons on her shirt near her neck, but didn't see it coming from her skin. "Hold still, I think I know where it's coming from." Dante reached his hand into the top pocket of her coat and pulled out a tiny shard. It slowly started to lose its glow, but carried a magnificent shine along its surface. "It's saphyres...but how?" Dante asked.

A long silence followed. "Evelyn," Alison said. "She placed it there."

"But how do you know?"

"I just do. I think she really does care, Dante."

Dante paused and looked around as if trying to see

if someone was following them and he whispered, "You were floating through the air...I think that the saphyres saved you."

"But how? How could this happen, there's no way I used the saphyres"

"But you did Alison, saphyres was founded with love and with love it gives back," Dante told her. It was the most beautiful thing she had ever heard Dante say. Tears started to flood her eyes and formed streams running down her cheeks. "We made it, Alison," Dante said and then hugged her. For some odd reason, even in that warm moment of reunion, Alison could only think about the dragon she had seen. *"Was it real?"* she thought. *"Was any of this real? The tears? The kingdom in the sky? Dante?"* She couldn't stop thinking about the possibility of all of this being fake. "Well, shall we?" Dante asked her. As Dante was holding her, Alison looked across his shoulder and was astonished at what she saw. The stone ledge was a path that twisted and turned in all directions. Vines and plants with gorgeous flowers blooming intertwined with the stone. The path looked ancient and seemed as if it hadn't been used for years.

Then she happened to look down and noticed his uncovered feet. "What happened to your shoes?"

"I lost one during the jump and decided walking around in one shoe wouldn't be very convenient," he responded. Alison saw that Dante and herself were slightly bruised and dirty from the landing. They both then looked up and couldn't even see the edge of the surface of Altaria. They had a great view of the sun as it was moments away from dying behind the horizon. "You know, no one has been down here since Altaria was first discovered."

"And how again was Altaria created?" she asked.

He looked at her and gave her a wink and a smile of outright happiness formed across his face. "I don't know, but whoever created such a place, well, they must have been true artists to make such a haven."

CHAPTER 15

THE HEART

"What's going on!" Alison yelled as Altaria began to shake again. Pieces of the stone that ran up the ground of Altaria began to break off and tumble toward them.

"Let's just find some shelter. There've gotta be some old mines around here somewhere," Dante responded as he grabbed her hand and took off running. It was now dawn and the terrain of the environment was slightly overwhelming, but magnificent. It reminded Alison of running through the fields and gardens with her father as a young girl. There were stones stacked on top of each other all around and vines meandered along the path covering the cracks. The shaking finally stopped and Dante and Alison came to a halt and sat down to recover their energy.

"It's like a lost city in ruins…" she said with a melancholy tone.

"Yeah, this is the oldest part of Altaria. I've only heard tales before, but now I'm seeing it with my own eyes."

"The vines…it's like a garden that's now ruined. Where do you think all this vegetation came from? There's nowhere for it to grow from?" Alison asked.

"I've been thinking about that since we fell and reached the ledge. The vines and shrubs seem to be coming out of the stone walls that border the outside and then grow even off the edge." Dante pointed toward the large cracked walls.

"What's going on?"

"I don't know, but whatever is causing this can't be good. Just look how the vegetation is growing up toward the surface," he said as the two of them continued to fight through the vegetation that covered everything. It was as if they were venturing into a deep forest. They came to an open stone platform that had pillars raised toward an old roof giving it support. It had patches of light shining through holes and seemed as if it was on its last leg. The place got darker and darker as they went on and the vines grew thicker.

"What could this place have been, Dante?"

"It looks like some kind of sanctuary. I remember

reading about the founding people of Altaria building sanctuaries for the harvest. It was tradition to preserve some of the saphyres in case of a lack of supply and they didn't want the saphyres to ever leave Altaria," he told her.

She was still very curious as Alison was losing sight ahead of her due to the darkness. They followed the path as it bent around a statue that was too torn apart to tell what it used to be. In the distance little lights started to appear, it was as if they were walking to the stars. "The lights, it looks like the shard!" Alison cried out with glee.

"And that's because they are…saphyres…Alison we've found it." Alison ran toward the light in excitement. "Wait! Stop, it could be a trap," Dante yelled and ran after her. As they both approached the lights from the saphyres, the place was illuminated greatly and all around they could see hundreds of openings to tunnels. They seemed to be everywhere and Alison was in awe at the sight. "So these are the great mines," Dante said.

"The saphyres…the tunnels…they're everywhere. How are we going to find the right way to go?"

But Dante didn't answer yet, as if he was deep in thought as he gazed downward and said "We have to be careful. This place wasn't supposed to ever be discovered again, why? I don't know, but Altaria has been mined from the surface for generations and still no one has ever come as close as you and I are now to the core."

"Dante, you're the one who's done it and no matter what happens, no matter what we find in there, I'm staying by your side," Alison said sincerely.

"So you do trust me? Good, because your trust is what I'm going to need. What we will find I don't know either, but I do know the core is somewhere nearby and one of these mines will lead us to it."

Alison just looked around in utter confusion. "Which one should we try?"

"Good question, Alison...good question. Luck is all we have. Just watch your step and stay close to me," he said and held out his hand toward Alison. "The shard please. I have an idea." Alison didn't question his request. She handed him the saphyres shard that was in her coat pocket which he took and set it down on a stone near his feet. He then walked over and picked up a nearby rock and set it down next to the shard. He picked a large leaf off of a vine and placed it flat on the stone, and then placed the shard on top of the leaf. "Saphyres is a little more fragile than you think. Now watch closely," and he took the rock with his right hand and smashed the little crystal of saphyres. Alison was horrified as her treasured saphryes shard was now not only shattered but reduced to dust, but true to her promise, she didn't say a word. "I used the leaf to catch the dust, which we're going to need," Dante told her. He carefully picked up the leaf with the saphyres dust and inhaled a strong breath of air and blew across the leaf like a mighty wind. The dust flew from the leaf straight toward the tunnels ahead. As alison watched, she was amazed to see it had scattered all around and was flying through every tunnel that she could see. Her eyes followed more dust particles as they made their way up where she could see more tunnels higher up, it was as if there was no end to them. The dust was like a wave of the ocean rushing to shore. It made the tunnels all around glow and Alison could see the trails until the light vanished far into the mines. "Just watch," Dante whispered. Alison wasn't sure if they were listening for some kind of noise, but the sound of her heart beating against her chest made the situation sound like a pack of horses was charging at them. Suddenly a slight bit of dust rushed out of one of the tunnel openings and twirled around them until it disintegrated into nothing. "That's the one we want," Dante said as he walked confidently toward the opening.

"How do you know?" she asked.

"Just a hunch. But I remember learning that the saphyres core that lies beneath the surface of Altaria was said to be so great, which must explain why these bits of saphyres are stuck all around us. The force is so great it lodged these pieces into the stone," he explained with certainty.

He took her by the hand and together they went into the mine where the dust had traveled out of. The little shards of saphyres that were stuck here and there provided just enough light for them to make their way through.

"It's hot as a furnace in here," Alison complained as she tasted the saltiness from her sweat dripping down her face. The air became scarce as they trudged on deeper into the mine. She stopped and took off her coat and hat and pulled her hair out of bind.

"Just what I was afraid of," Dante said as he also stopped and planted his feet together and gazed forward.

Alison walked up right next to him. "Give me a break, what's wrong now?" she asked. Dante didn't respond, but Alison soon realized the problem. "Split path huh?" she whispered.

"Well, I guess it's either one or the other, but something just doesn't add up. The saphyres is lodged into stone and now this…I can't think of any reason the people who mined would stop mining one direction, come back to this point and then start digging in a different direction," Dante said in a skeptical tone.

"Maybe they could cover more mining this way."

"I beg to differ. The idea was to go in one complete direction until you hit stone that couldn't be dug past or they reached the core. That's why the tunnel entrances only appear from back at the sanctuary," Dante explained as he was struggling to think of their next move. "Left has always been lucky for me, so shall we?"

"And since when has the left path in life been lucky for you?" Alison teased.

"Haven't thought that far…but anyways let's get a move on," he said as he started toward the left entrance. Alison pulled her hand back and just stood there watching him as she thought, "*It can't be this easy, can it?*" "Well hurry up, won't you," he called back to her and true to her word, Alison moved forward following him deep into the mine. The mine's stone was dark black like coal. The temperature had suddenly begun to drop and was now nice and cool. The air freshened up and reminded Alison of the spring with its cool breeze. "That breeze has to be coming from somewhere, and just look, there're more vines up ahead," Dante groaned as he pointed forward. Up ahead there were vines and small shrubs with tiny sprouts of some kind of flower poking out of them. "Wait…stay here. I'll be back," Dante commanded as they came to a halt. He swiftly ran ahead to a wall in front of them that was densely decorated in the vines. With his hands he began moving the vines to the side and ripping the shrubs away, digging out the vines as if he were looking for buried treasure. He stopped suddenly and kept his eyes fixed on something he found. "Alison, come here. You need to see this, but don't worry they've been dead for ages." Alison felt her heart sink as he said the word "dead" and knew what he had found was not good. She slowly moved towards him and knelt down.

Tangled in the pile of vines in a large space between the stone laid two skeletons.

"What happened!" Alison exclaimed.

"Just look at their uniforms. There's no way they could have been miners. Their uniforms are that of Altaria guardians." Dante had a very disturbed look on his face. With his hand he brushed away the cobwebs that stuck to the skulls. "There's only one reason they had these here," Dante said now with anger and fear in his voice. Alison remained silent and was becoming anxious. "Poison gas…these are masks to prevent you from inhaling the poison," he said as he took both masks off the skulls of the guard's skeletons. "It's a trap," Dante whispered as if he knew destiny had stabbed him in the back.

Alison didn't know what to say and barely understood the conclusion Dante was getting at. "Poison?" she asked.

"We're not just going into a mine, Alison. We're heading straight into a grave of poison. Wherever these vines lead, it can't be good. The air is picking up here and that must be why this poison is here," Dante said. "Here let's quickly put these on," he told her as he handed her one of the brown rugged masks. They were very strange, but unique looking. Alison had never seen such a thing. They seemed to have been made of some kind of animal fur, Alison thought. A piece strapped to a small sheet of glass to look out went around the mouth and nose and eyes.

"It's pretty tight." Talking with the mask on was quite strange to her as there was a slight echo when she talked.

"Good. It's supposed to be. They had these for a reason and whatever is up ahead…well, let's just say we're going into the eye of the storm…a poisoned one that is," Dante said and then didn't say another word. He led Alison along with him down the path slowly, watching every step they made.

"What is that?!" Alison pointed as they approached spurs growing on the walls and colorful spotted mushrooms growing all over. Alison then put herself directly behind Dante and jumped as one of the spurs bursted into dust and floated around them.

"Boy, it's a good thing we have these masks," he told her. As they ventured on they noticed the glowing saphyres in the walls were larger pieces and shed more light.

"Dante, look out!" Alison yelled, and Dante without even looking at the danger, quickly rolled forward on the path and escaped a shard of saphyres that fell from the ceiling.

"We're walking into a mine of traps. Just look." Dante pointed at what appeared to be a vine, but was actually a green rope used to spring the trap. "Let me go first from here out. I'm sure there's going to be more of this." Alison was about to object, but Dante waved his hand in front of her to be silent. He crouched down over near the right wall where there were three large roots growing in a strange formation. He saw something shining from the center area which was hollow behind the roots. It was a different sparkle, unlike the saphyres. He reached into the hollow part and grabbed hold of something. Alison just stood and watched him tug at it without interfering herself. "Come on, come on," he muttered. "There!" Dante cried out. He acted as if he had found treasure, but instead pulled out a small sword. Alison gave him a look like he was the strangest, but bravest warrior she had ever met. "Now this will come in handy. If we're going into battle we best be prepared."

"Don't bother with the whole brave lecture yet, Mr. Hero. By the looks of it we have a ways to go."

"That may be so, but we've gone far enough for now and barely escaped death."

"Barely escaped? Your reaction back there was remarkable!"

"That's because I have eyes on the back of my head." Dante laughed at his own statement as he sat softly on some kind of stump growing out of the ground. He took the blade and gazed at the dullness of its edge. "Now what kind of being would wield this in such a place? Looks like you've seen some action my friend." Dante spoke to the sword as if it were alive.

Alison, too, sat down opposite of Dante. "Roots,

vines...it's like a dungeon of the poisoned forest down here," Alison commented as a current of air drifted past them along with a nasty, poisonous gas. It was a yellow and brown color that looked like sulfur. "Gross. These spurs are the most toxic thing I've ever seen. How could anyone have ever made it down here?"

"That's just it. I don't know if anyone ever actually made it to the core," Dante replied.

"Then how do you, or anyone for that matter, know there even is a core?"

"I thought you'd probably ask that...well to tell you the truth it's more of a myth than something actually witnessed, but we do have good reason to believe there is a large saphyres core at the center beneath Altaria." Alison was puzzled and placed her head against her knees. She murmured something to herself as if she had lost hope. "What did you say?" Dante asked her. She looked up, but couldn't keep her own eyes on him as she felt ashamed for feeling defeated.

"I feel, Dante...I feel like we're just chasing a dream," she told him.

"He didn't respond right away as he went into deep thought about how he would respond to such a thing. "And you haven't been chasing a dream of your own, Alison?" Alison couldn't believe what Dante had asked. She felt it was an arrogant assumption.

"You don't know me that well, and the dream I'm

chasing is exactly that very word."

"And what is that?"

"A dream, just a dream…and dreams aren't real, none of this in fact, no matter how much I want it to be, no matter how amazing Altaria and everything you've shown me about adventure…my life is surrounded by reality and in reality I am nothing, and being nothing is boring and there is no room for dreams," Alison replied, and to her revelation she sounded just like her mother.

"Dreams are what I thrive on, Alison, and you should too. Whether what is or isn't real, none of that matters. It is an art to dream no matter what, and those dreams in your heart will lead you to bigger things, Alison. You just gotta believe." Alison could barely make out the words Dante said as they became faint and so was she. It felt like her soul was drifting apart from her body and that she was falling back into another dimension. "Alison?" Dante called to her. "Alison!!!" his voice came again in a cry for help. Alison fainted and darkness covered her eyes and even her mind.

CHAPTER 16

WHEN DREAMS COME TRUE

"The Rainbow Road," Alison read aloud on the sign in front of her. The sign was old and rusted. It had symbols on it as if it were some kind of ancient language, but Alison could read it fluently. There before her, going miles and miles far into the distance was a road that looked like glass stained with color. "*Colors of the rainbow,*" she thought as she looked at the sign and then at the path in front of her. It was bright and there was an eerie mist surrounding the outside of the road as if the road went through a field of clouds.

Alison looked and behold there was a marking on the red color of the road. This time she couldn't understand what it meant and then she saw there were other markings that were similar. Without doubt that there was danger ahead she made her way along the rainbow road. She noticed that her shoes were gone, but her feet felt smooth against the road as if she were walking on the waves at sea.

The path became narrower the further she went and the silence was peaceful and to Alison it was quite exhilarating. It was as if she had found the path to something beyond a dream and into a realm of tranquility. After walking far, she didn't grow the least bit tired. She then started to stumble across leafy vines covered with flowers surrounding her like a garden. The vines were very lush and flowed with the sways of color that patterned the rainbow road. It started to seem as if she stepped through time as the further she went the more shadows appeared on the road and vines and flowers were rotting as if the life had been drained from them. Cracks shaped like lightning bolts crossed from one side to the other on the path.

"*I can't stop moving!*" Alison thought to herself and then finally shouted it out loud. "I can't stop moving!" Her legs kept trudging on and even though she tried resisting, her body insisted for her to keep moving down the path.

She came to the point where all the vegetation was dead. The vines were dry, dark and shriveled up. The vines turned into roots the further she went. The roots became thicker and thicker until they were so big they formed an arch-like shelter above her.

"Wait...no!" she yelled trying to resist again. The frightening roots had no end it seemed and it felt as if she were walking into the mouth of a great beast. She could hear the roots begin to bend and twist making a bone crushing noise.

Alison then felt something crawl around her ankle and it slowly coiled up her leg. It was a vine that sprouted out of the ground and it stopped her from moving forward. The vine continued to grow larger, like the roots. She was able to grab hold of the vine and she ripped it apart until her ankle was free.

At last Alison had gained full control of her body and she ran as fast as she could back in the direction she had come. She swung her arms at the same speed of her legs, pushing herself to get away from the roots. She looked behind her for an instant and saw the roots creeping out of the rainbow road and shattering the path behind her.

The roots surged after Alison like a pack of wolves. Adrenaline was powering her as it rushed through her veins, but she felt that she wasn't getting any closer to the entrance of the road. "You're not getting me this time!" she yelled back at the roots raging through the road and collapsing it into pieces that drifted away.

Suddenly the path beneath shattered and she lost all control of her body. Alison's eyes widened with the shock of fear as vines from the darkness below wrapped around her arms and legs and pulled her into the abyss. Her right arm had just enough strength to reach out. "Where are you taking me?" Alison breathlessly whispered softly.

"To the depth of your fear," a voice boomed from the shadow abyss. Alison closed her eyes and relaxed her mind. She felt a tranquil state sink into her soul. "Then to the depth I'll go," she replied to the unknown. It was as if she let go of every ounce of energy she had and gave in to her captor.

"If you won't get up, I'll have to carry you," Dante shouted as he picked up Alison's body and carried her on his shoulder. The ground beneath them, as well as the rest of Altaria, was shaking more violently than ever. Dante ran while carrying Alison deeper into the mine. "*Let's stop a minute,*" he said to himself, and to Alison, "Come on, snap out of it," as he carefully tried to set her down against the wall.

"We have to go back; it's going to the surface!" Alison yelled as she opened her eyes and kicked for Dante to let go.

He held onto her and kept her on the ground where she sat. "No, Alison we can't. What's wrong with you anyways?" he asked and all of a sudden part of the stone ceiling collapsed. The rocks piled up in large shards and saphyres landed on the ground around their feet and shattered into dust. Alison and Dante coughed as the dust circulated the atmosphere of the mine.

Alison then ran to the pile of rubble blocking their exit. "How are we going to get out now!" Alison panicked as she tried moving the boulders of stone, but they didn't budge. There was only a small opening they could see through to the other side. She tried squeezing through, only to hurt herself in the attempt.

"Just save your strength; we're not getting out that way."

"Oh, yeah, and how else are we getting out? You aren't even trying over here," Alison said with anguish.

Dante looked forward and was only determined to get closer to the core. "Doesn't matter; we still need to find that core. Getting back is the least of our concerns right now." Alison was shocked to hear his unconcerned reaction. She started to feel fragile, almost like broken glass. The weakness concerned Alison and she began pacing slowly.

"There's no time for this. We've made it this far. Follow me to the core and we can get out of this hole, I promise." He tried to reassure her, but she acted as if she wasn't listening and gave off the impression that she was in deep thought. Alison thought back to the rainbow road and the roots growing from beneath it.

She then broke from her trance and turned to Dante. "Do you still have that stone? The one you use to start a fire?" she asked.

"Yes? But there's no sense in starting a fire; we can

already see with saphyres everywhere."

"Just give it to me. I need to show you something," Alison replied and held out her hand. He gave her the stone and Alison walked over to the nearest wall. She stood in silence for a moment with her eyes closed and placed the stone against a smooth area of the wall. With her eyes still closed, she began to draw something. She moved her hand with the stone swiftly against the surface, not peeking a bit to see what the image was.

Dante stood in wonder at first as he watched Alison outline something, and he soon picked up on what it was. A chill ran up his spine as he thought, *"How did she know?"*

Alison turned around rapidly. "Dante, what does this mean?" she asked while pointing at the symbol she just drew.

"Altaria," he replied while wiping the sweat from his forehead. "It means Altaria," he said again.

Alison dropped the stone and felt the image of the rainbow road cloud her mind once again. "The symbol on the road means 'Altaria?' But why?" She then closed her eyes and visioned the road from a bottom view and could see the roots growing rapidly up and over the surface of the rainbow road. The symbols on the road began to glow. This time Alison wasn't on the path herself, but instead was watching it from all around. She noticed a symbol in the center of the path that was slightly larger than the other symbols. She couldn't interpret it, but knew it was significant. Vines began to grow like branches from the symbol and Alison could feel her view of the symbol drifting away as if it was being pulled away from her memory. She tried desperately to somehow link the connection between the symbol and the one that meant 'Altaria.' Roots then suddenly grew from the bottom of the symbol and vines formed out of the top; the 'Altaria' symbol appeared and that's when it hit Alison like a wave of truth unlocking the very thing buried that they had been looking for. Alison opened her eyes to leave her vision and placed her attention on Dante.

"Well, in case you're wondering, you zoned out again," he said, but Alison didn't respond as she tried pulling herself back together.

"The Hollow tree..." Alison said softly. Her eyes were watery and Dante could see that she was disturbed about something.

"What are you talking about? Don't let this place get to you. If we keep moving I know we can get out of here. The miners had to make a backup..."

"It's been here this whole time. Your city, this kingdom is heading for destruction and it started from the roots," Alison interrupted, but Dante didn't understand. "Dante the tree! All of this, it's from the tree!" she yelled and then suddenly more spurs sprayed into the air with viscous gases. With this Dante knew another disturbance in the ground was about to take place, so he grabbed Alison by the hand and ran further into the mine. The gases became heavy and mushrooms were now sprouting out of the many roots along the path. Dante stopped suddenly and looked all around at the roots below them. His mask kept fogging and he tried clearing it, but the vegetation was becoming too overwhelming.

"It's a tree…one big tree, but why is it growing through Altaria?" Dante asked in desperation to know the answer.

"I saw the symbol, 'Altaria.' The branches were growing out of the symbol and then this appeared." She then picked up Dante's stone she had used before and yet again drew another symbol on the wall. "This time I'm sure of what it means," she said. Dante's eyes were wide open and he couldn't believe what he was seeing. "It means hollow doesn't it?" Dante's attention started to turn into rage and he felt like he was trapped in a conspiracy. "Hollow tree…it's going to turn Altaria hollow from the ground up, Dante," Alison warned.

"If that's true then there really must be a core," he told her.

"But how? What could have started this? Has the tree really been here your whole life or even as long as Altaria has been around?"

"It was here before I came into this world, but something evil must have been planted here and that evil has found a way to harness the power of saphyres and that tree..." Dante paused. "That tree...I...I mean, we... called it home," he said and sadly looked down. Dante stood near the bright glow of the saphyres in the walls. Alison could see just how worn out he was by the cuts and scrapes on his arms and legs. His feet were covered with dirt and his face was drenched in sweat and dust. "Well, I think we could both use a bath right about now," Dante said and laughed a little. Alison could tell he was sore and his laughter only caused pain in his chest. All of a sudden they heard a noise come from the stone above them. "This can't be good, no way back, only forward, Alison, and I know we can make it," Dante said with much more courage than he felt. Slowly small roots began to break through the stone above them and creep down towards their heads.

"Alright, let's get out of here!" Alison yelled and this time it was she who grabbed Dante by the hand and led him down the mine. The mine started to become more narrow and by now there was no stone to see as the vegetation had covered every bit of the rock. "Look, the shards of saphyres are in the vines," Alison pointed out.

"It's taking over all the saphyres and soon there won't be any left for Altaria to stay afloat, its deteriorating from the inside out," he replied. The path was now like the heart of a jungle. Alison struggled to step over the vines and roots growing in all directions. She tried ducking under a bundle of long snake like vines that hung down. As she reached the other side she felt a sharp tug on the mask across her face. It was too late for her to hang on to it as the mask was stripped from her face and fell to ground and was soon taken in by the roots.

"Dante!" she yelled and quickly held her hand up to her nose to stop her breathing.

"Your mask! What happened?" Alison just shook her head. She couldn't hold her breath any longer and finally let go. She tried not to take in deep breaths, but to her surprise she was okay. "Alison I..."

"It's alright, I'm fine...look."

"That was a close one," he replied as he too took off his mask. "I guess we're safe from the spurs, but we're getting closer. It's like we're walking into the mouth of a great beast." Dante's words took Alison by surprise as she thought back to the roots that formed an enormous mouth like that of a beast on the rainbow road. "Take my hand. I'll help you through this." She grabbed hold of his hand and could feel a profound level of heat in his palms. "We will help each other get through this." Dante looked into her eyes and knew he was seeing a side of Alison he never knew.

CHAPTER 17

WHERE HEARTS MEET

Dante slashed with the blade he drew from his coat at the vines that entangled them. "They're growing faster!" Alison called out to him.

"I realize that, it's just too thick in here." Dante could barely keep hold of the sword which was now so dull he had to saw his way through. "I've found a way through, but we're going to have to go one at a time. I'll hold back the vines and when I say to, crawl as far as you can until you reach the other side."

"The other side of what?" Alison asked hastily.

"Just go. I'll be right behind you." Dante put his back to the vines swirling out of the walls and ceiling to hold them back.

Alison got down on her hands and knees and tried desperately to crawl. She could hardly see in front of her, but trusted what Dante said and just knew there was some obstruction in the way to get around. She used her hands to guide her way through and at first all she could feel was vines, but then her arms reached an open space and the air inside was filled with a cold temptation. It was an energy that felt like pure serenity. She finally made her way into the open area. It was enormous and the whole place was illuminated as if she were standing directly on a star. She reached back into the opening she had just come from and tried to find Dante making his way through. "Dante where are you?" she called out.

"Right here!" Dante yelled back as he stumbled and crawled with rage as the vines were attempting to overcome him. "Alison!" Dante yelled. He was stuck in the crawl space as the vines attached to his body and wrapped tightly around his torso.

"I've got you, just a little more," Alison said trying to rip the vines away to free Dante.

"I'm too late. Take this and get out of here. Find a way to Jasper and tell him the core is here."

Alison turned in a state of surprise. Tears streamed down her face as she felt her thrilled spirit begin to drain from herself. "I'm not letting you go," she cried. "We've come too far together to ever let go!"

"That's okay, Alison. You haven't let go, you've

brought me to a place in myself I've never been to and if there was ever time for me to go…well let's just say I'm happy," Dante said as his hand slipped out of Alison's and he was gone. He was pulled in by the vines as Alison watched him disappear.

"No! Dante!" Alison screamed. Her cry for him echoed all around until it died in the distance. The place was now quiet. Alison kept her head down low as she rose from her knees. She was speechless and watched as her tears splashed on the back of her hands then plunged to the ground. It was then that she then noticed the blade Dante had been wielding earlier lying on the cool stone ground in front of her. She gazed at the streak of light reflecting off the blades surface and realized that she couldn't leave Dante. She then picked it up and turned around to face the light. "Hello," she called out. The bright light began to slightly dim and now Alison could see what it was that looked like a star. "Saphyres," she said softly. Suddenly the ground shook and she heard a shattering noise like bones were being broken.

"Alison!" came Dante's voice as his head and shoulders emerged from the small opening.

She ran to his aid and as she placed her hand out, Dante threw his hand in hers. "Dante! I didn't want to let you go, you're here and alive…and I…"

"Alison, it's okay, save your breath," Dante interrupted as he came out into the open. His shirt was torn to shreds and blood was dripping like soft tears from his chest.

"You're hurt, just let me..." Dante placed his hand over her mouth before she could finish. He slowly took it away as she became quiet. He continued to look into her beautiful eyes that he always admired. With her in his arms he leaned forward with the very little energy he had left and kissed her on her delicate lips. Alison had never been taken by such surprise in her entire life, but then in that moment her spirit held back any fear, shyness. She had never felt something so warm touching her heart and releasing love through her veins. Alison suddenly pulled her head back as she heard a scraping noise coming from behind Dante. They both turned to look and saw a vine stretching out and pulling the sword toward the vine-ridden walls. "Dante the sword," she cried out. But as soon as they stood up, the vine pulled the blade up the wall and it was sucked in abruptly. It was as if the walls were alive and hungered for anything and everything.

"Don't worry. We're fine without it," Dante reassured her and turned his attention to the glow. "So this is it, huh? Saphyres you've been here all along and this is your sanctuary...the quiet resting place." Dante's words were strong and Alison could tell he knew the danger wasn't over. She looked around and saw the largest roots connecting to the saphyres core. The core itself was marvelous, it looked like an enormous diamond dazzling before them.

"What do we do now, Mr Hero?"

"Well, I guess I hadn't got that far in my plan, but by the looks of it, the core has sure lost a great deal," he told her. Dante then noticed that in this room there were no more shards in the walls and no exits he could see. "Now how is this possible? This room is quite impressive, I must admit, but the makeup is quite confusing."

"I think I've been here before," Alison whispered to herself.

"What? Alison tell me again what you said, I need to know!"

"The tree, it's above ground here. I know it is. We're right under it!"

"Alison, tell me now what happened when you saw this place with your eyes." Dante told her as he gazed fiercely right in her eyes and placed both hands on her shoulders.

"I remember a tree and vines and the roots grew and everything was dark while evil roamed all through the land. But I...I know this place because the saphyres has been running through the roots and giving it great power. The roots were always connected to a shimmering light in the distance," she told him as her mind flashed back to the haunting visions she'd had since the beginning of it all.

"The saphyres, we've got to shut it down," Dante replied abruptly.

"Destroy it? But that will bring Altaria down with it!"

"Not destroy, but stop its bind with these roots. If what I'm thinking is right, then the tree grew from the core and it's full of poison to not only ruin Altaria, but acquire the energy Altaria survives on."

Alison was speechless from his words and didn't know what to expect to happen next. Without giving much thought she turned to Dante. "Why spend your lives here? Your people can come down to Earth, my home…our land it's…" she said, but Dante interrupted her.

"It's not that easy Alison…ouch." Dante quickly placed his hand on his left torso after feeling a sharp pain. He twitched a little as he started to remove his worn shirt. Alison saw red drops of blood fall from his body and Dante grew cold as he moved more than he should have.

"Dante…it's a piece of saphyres," Alison spoke softly as she dashed over and knelt down at his side. A shard of saphyres was lodged into his flesh. The piece happened to glow brighter than most.

"Wow, I guess I didn't feel that one right away," Dante chuckled.

"We have to get you out of here. I'll take care of the core," Alison told him.

"Do you know how to stop it?" Dante asked in a quiet tone.

"No, but I'm sure you had something up your sleeve,"

she replied.

Dante lifted up his arms which were dirty and bruised. "No sleeves my dear...not much left at all..." His energy began collapse within him; his voice grew faint and he stuttered for words.

"Dante, we can get out of here. We can tell the others and find a way through this," Alison said and held Dante closer.

"Not today Alison...today it all ends," he told her. The shard in his torso began to glow as bright as the core. He grabbed hold of the shard and with a mighty force pulled it out. Alison fell to the ground beside him, speechless, wide eyed, watching him. Dante refused to give in to the pain; the shard was completely out of him and then he stood straight up with a firm stance. He didn't yell in agony or flinch in fear. "Now it's my turn to end this all!" he yelled. "This tree grew with the power of saphyres and with saphyres I'm going to send it back from where it came!" Dante yelled at the top of his lungs and ran toward the bright core and without stopping he used the shard to strike the main root attached to the core with all his remaining strength. He retreated back to Alison hopping on one foot. Alison could tell he was really feeling the pain now and once again rushed to his aid. The roots spiraled out of control around the core with the shard stuck in it. The glow from the core now became brighter than ever before, so bright Alison and

Dante could no longer see it as they were blinded by the light. "It's done...I think it's done...I hope..." Dante said, gasping for words.

"Let's get you out of here! Where is the way out?" Alison asked looking around, desperate to get them back to the surface.

The ground shook again and the roots grew swiftly from the stone ceiling above and creeped down the walls forming a barrier. Dante didn't respond, he took his arm off Alison's shoulder and picked up a small piece of saphyres off the ground. Without asking for the stone Alison was holding onto, he reached into her pocket and took it out. Alison was speechless and frozen as she noticed the blood rushing down his chest and his arms. He took the stone and with it he crushed the saphyres, turning it into dust. He scooped the dust in his palm and began to blow softly. Alison forgot all about the roots and ground erupting. It was as if time suddenly stopped as the dust danced in the current of the air and sparkled like nothing she had ever seen. Dante held his hand out slowly and the dust then swiftly went to the surrounding walls of the core sanctuary. A small glow came about from the dust and it formed a light barrier that stopped the roots from reaching the ground. Then a collection of dust formed and went straight toward a large crack in the stone wall behind the core. The stone erupted and broke down into a pile of rock.

"Come on, I've found our way out!" Dante exclaimed who now seemed to have much of his energy back.

"But how did you do that?!" she asked.

"I too had a vision and mine was getting out of here," he told her. Alison smiled and knew there is a vision for everything and on this path there never is an end.

ALISON OF ALTARIA

Dante let Alison go ahead of him. The path they were now following was quite narrow, but they knew they had been through worse. Alison kept thinking she could see the light of day, but a vision kept appearing mysteriously in her mind. "Honestly, I don't know where this is taking us, but I'm relying on hope to get us out," Dante said as they ran.

Alison knew she couldn't let him keep running on his own strength or he would bleed more. "I'm helping you through this," and pulled his arm up around her shoulder.

"But I can make it…I'm fine."

"No buts. I'm getting you out of here and that's final," Alison declared just as they heard a rumbling above their heads that sounded like a boulder rushing down a mountain. A crack formed above them and raced in the direction they had been going and the ground shook along with it.

Back on the surface of Altaria, the guards of the kingdom of Altaria formed in a prestigious line along the wall bordering the city. The city continued to shake, but the guards stood firm.

Evelyn, along with some guards, trotted up the stone bridge leading to one end of the wall. "Hold your ground and prepare yourselves. Today an hour has come and we must defend this kingdom till the last man!" Evelyn shouted from the highest point of the wall to the guards.

The quiet corners of the city then erupted from underneath as the large roots breached the ground at last. The army of guards on the wall quickly turned around and held their position. They raised their long spears and others pulled back the strings of their bow. "Zar, tell your men to hold until I give my signal," Evelyn said.

Zar nodded and put his fist in the air to prepare the signal.

The roots spiraled as if a giant was crawling from the earth. Evelyn's eyes were wide open with fear and she could feel her heart pounding against her chest. She was about to give the signal, but suddenly the roots stopped moving just before reaching the heart of the city.

The people of the city all around panicked, but didn't

come out of hiding, as they had previously been warned to stay indoors. The ground stopped shaking and dead silence followed. Suddenly the giant roots began to turn dark and slowly started to shrink.

Evelyn watched in amazement; she was utterly confused at what was happening before her. The roots retreated slowly toward the hole in the ground they came out of, but stopped short. They were now rotting quickly and then suddenly they burst into sparkling dust. A wind came and swirled the dust around until little shards fell to the ground.

"Saphyres!" Evelyn yelled. The guards didn't know what to think, but they still stood their ground. "They did it after all..." Evelyn whispered. The sun was at its highest peak of the day and Evelyn couldn't remember the last time she had seen the sky around so blue. "Zar, tell the men to stand down; it's over," Evelyn ordered.

"What happened, maam? Were we under attack?" Zar asked.

"Just tell everyone to stand down, there's no battle here," she replied. The guards all lowered their weapons and prepared to descend the wall into the city below. "Well, they actually did it after all," she spoke softly to herself. In the distant sky, Evelyn could see clouds forming together as darkness began to fall. She knew what would be coming and decided to find shelter to rest her weary self.

The bottom of Altaria continued to crumble. Alison and Dante were approaching the light they had seen at the end of the mine. "Looks like we may have to jump once again Alison and trust the fall."

"But we're at the very bottom of Altaria. There's nothing else to catch us and not to mention I don't have the shard anymore," she said in a worried tone.

"Looks like we need a miracle once again," Dante said and was still confident; however, the light at the end suddenly vanished as something gigantic blocked its path. At first neither Dante nor Alison could tell what was covering the opening, but as they came closer, Dante recognized it as something quite familiar. "Majesty!" he shouted and Dante threw up his hands and yelled with excitement.

"I don't think Evelyn has come to rescue us, Dante," Alison called out as she tried to keep up.

"No, I mean, my ship...The Majesty!" he exclaimed and then picked up his pace even more. He held Alison's hand tighter, dragging her along as he looked back and saw the stones piling up behind them, trying to outrun the disaster. "Once again, when I say jump, you do it and whatever you do, don't look down." Alison looked into his eyes with far less fear than ever.

"There they are; pull the ship in as close as you can!" Jasper yelled to the others as The Majesty sailed forward, trying to make its way to them.

"We will see just how close we can get this old thing. Here goes nothing," Laboo responded as he took the wheel of The Majesty and rotated it hard to the left. The ship pulled hard to its side, the winds were strong, but they had hoped to beat it anyways.

Marcy and The Apothecary were at the front bow of the ship. Marcy saw them approaching the ledge and knew they had no time to spare. "Jump for it, you two! We will catch you at all cost!" she shouted to Alison and Dante. The Apothecary was standing still next to Marcy. He quickly set down a bag he was holding and reached his hand out as well to help them.

"Alison, don't look down...Jump!" Dante yelled. He took Alison's hand and gave her a boost up where she was caught by The Apothecary. He pulled her into the ship and set her safely down. Dante was still in danger, he jumped, but couldn't get off the ground far enough. Just short of Marcy's hands, he fell downwards, but managed to grab hold of a rope on the lower bow.

"Hang on, Dante. The ship can't hold here any longer, but I'll pull you in," Marcy shouted down to him. The winds were rough and finally pulled the ship into the current and it slowly drifted away.

Surprisingly Dante wasn't struggling to hold on. He was quite relaxed and watched as the mines created by the founders of Altaria collapsed. The bottom of Altaria crumbled to pieces and fell to the Earth down below.

"Well, looks like Altaria lost a good chunk of its base, but it'll manage, as long as saphyres thrives," Dante said to himself, though his words were carried through the wind and were heard by everyone on The Majesty. There was a loud rumble that followed as more stone fell and then there was silence as Marcy pulled on the rope and hoisted Dante up to the deck. "Alison…where is she?"

"She's over there." Marcy pointed to where The Apothecary was taking care of her. "Dante you're hurt." Marcy stated in a sympathetic voice.

Dante looked down at his bare chest and torso and saw that he was no longer bleeding, but severely bruised. "I've been through worse, Marcy…I've been through worse." Dante then walked over to Alison who was lying down on the deck where The Apothecary was tending to her wounds.

"Now I know why you all call him The Apothecary," Alison said to Dante as he was standing over her watching The Apothecary treat her.

"He's good at what he does, I'll say that. Saved me quite a few times, in fact," Dante said with a grin. The Apothecary once again did not speak, he just nodded to the both of them.

"It must get tiring wearing that mask all day," Alison said softly to The Apothecary. He pulled tight on a stitch to close Alison's wound; it made her body jerk with pain. "Ouccchhh!" she cried out. The Apothecary stopped as he had finished healing her.

"Good as new," Laboo said as he walked to the front of the ship alongside Jasper who had a big smile on his face.

"Now this is a view I haven't seen for some time," Jasper said.

"We haven't been together as a team for quite some time," Laboo responded.

Alison got up carefully as she was still sore. She gazed around and noticed the light reflecting off each one of them. They wore magnificent armor that made the crew look like true warriors. Alison looked down at her ragged clothes and didn't feel so beautiful. "Don't worry. I know what you're thinking; we'll get you something new to wear," Marcy told her as she walked over to comfort her.

After Dante and Alison changed into new clothes, Dante felt more like himself and Alison had found a beautiful dress that matched her eyes. She felt more power and freedom in that moment than living her life in royalty. For an instant she thought about home and was surprised she hadn't thought about her mother or the land she was from. But maybe home just couldn't compare to the place she was at right now, not only in the sky, but also in her heart. As they sailed back to Altaria, they didn't dock. Marcy and the rest of the gang stood in a line along the side of the ship facing Altaria. Alison could see the great bravery in each one's eyes as they were prepared for any consequences that could come their way. "Well, Dante...Alison, it's been real...Alison you take care of yourself. I see that Dante has truly shown you a dream worth having," Jasper said in words that were sincere, but those very words actually pierced Alison quite deeply. The word "dream" appeared once again in her mind. She didn't know how to respond as her mind couldn't figure out the puzzle before her. She gave Jasper a hug and the rest of them and told them goodbye.

"Dante, I'm sure we'll be seeing you around," Laboo said.

"Possibly Laboo, you just never know, the skies are my true home," Dante replied back.

"You two...well, I'm not going to get all emotional here, but it's been some kind of fun," Marcy said and the rest laughed as they saw tears leak from her eyes.

The Apothecary walked out of line over to Dante and Alison. He held Alison's hand and opened it and then placed something in her palm. He closed her hand so no one else could see. "Keep this with you; it will be an angel when you need it most," The Apothecary told her. Alison couldn't believe his sweet and serene words and it was the first time she had ever heard him speak. She then peeked into her hand to see what it was he had given her. *"A dried herb?"* she thought. Dante tried not to peek, but saw over her shoulder at what it was. A grin swept across his face and he thought to himself *"Alison, you have no idea."*

The ship was close to Altaria, but still several feet away. "Well, here we go!" Marcy yelled.

"But wait, we're not close enough!" Alison shouted back. The gang each took a rope and swung to the ledge on Altaria and each one landed gracefully. It was the most incredible thing Alison had ever seen. They turned around for an instant to wave and then jumped to another ledge and ran toward the heart of Altaria.

"I guess I really owe them one, huh?" Dante said to Alison and laughed. They were the only ones left on the ship as the sun was back on the horizon. "Well, it's sundown and I guess we should be on our way," he told her. Alison wanted to ask where they were going next, but somehow just knew and kept quiet.

Dante turned and walked across the deck over to the captain's wheel. Alison stayed put and then started to turn to go to Dante until something caught her eye and she stopped. The clouds roamed in front of her view, but she could still see Altaria in the distance. On the top of the highest peak, she could see someone standing, looking upon them as they sailed away. In that moment Alison knew who it was and wasn't the least bit surprised, but what really impressed her was when she saw a hand wave. *"Evelyn, I never got the privilege to get to know who you really are, but you have a special place in your heart for love, I just know it,"* Alison thought to herself as Evelyn turned away and disappeared behind the clouds that had floated by and hid Altaria from view. She turned and saw Dante carefully steering the ship and she could tell he was proud to be where his title placed him, "Dante of the Skies." "Well, Mr. Hero, I'm going to assume our work here is not done yet," Alison called to him.

Dante smiled and closed his eyes for a bit. "The wind is just right Alison...do you think you have it in you for one last adventure?" he asked.

"I'll follow you wherever you sail," she replied with a laugh. Dante turned the wheel sharply and The Majesty sailed into the sunset. Time felt like a race in Alison's mind as she had the feeling that she'd been gone longer than she'd expected. Although she couldn't help but think of the word she wouldn't let seep into her mind - "dream." But she came to the fact that "reality" and "dream" were unknown on the adventure she was on. Alison wanted to accept that she may never know or even remember any of this, but hoped this time it wasn't her imagination, but the imagination of life itself.

CHAPTER 19

THE WINDOW

The dark clouds caught up to The Majesty. Then came rain and thunder. Dante was able to keep The Majesty under control and knew she was strong. Alison was on the deck letting her hair blow in the wind, not bothered one bit by the storm. "You're going to catch a cold in this rain," Dante shouted to her as the thunder roared through the sky.

Alison gave him a look like she could handle the weather. "Tell me something, Dante," Alison said as she left the rail and approached him at the captain's wheel. She searched inside herself for courage to ask him. "So where do we go from here?"

"From here? Well, Alison the night is ours, so I say

let's live in the moment," Dante replied. By now night had fallen and the moon was full. Its bright glow illuminated the ship and reflected off Alison's eyes as Dante couldn't take his off of them. "You really are something, Alison."

"Oh yeah? Well, I wasn't anything before you came."

"Don't say that. No matter what it was like at home, you're still your own person, Alison, and not to mention there's no one in the entire kingdom of Altaria that is as great as you are."

Alison then blushed and turned away from him to hide it. She couldn't take the big smile off of her face as she was happier than ever. "I do have one last request to ask you, Mr. Hero."

"Well, tonight, allow me to honor whatever request you have," Dante replied in a fancy tone.

Alison laughed at his humor and turned to face him. "Will you take me up in the crow's nest like you did before?"

Dante smiled and wouldn't let it go. "Of course," he said and led her up to the top where the crow's nest was and stood behind and put his hands on her shoulders.

"You know what's funny? This was my favorite part of this whole journey," she said as she held her arms out and gazed over the edge at the world down below. She felt like a bird that could fly anywhere in the world. Together they gazed up at the stars that were glowing bright above their heads and treasured every second that went by. "I'm going home aren't I?" Alison asked, but then thought *"What if this really is just a dream, they never do last...do they?"*

"I know what you're thinking Alison, but I don't want to interfere with your mind. You see, this whole time I have felt your struggles to bare what you have seen. I can show you many things, Alison, but never will I interfere with someone's thoughts. What you have seen will always be in your heart, just know that and hold onto it."

Dante's words really pursued Alison as she thought *"He didn't say no?"* She felt her eyes start to shut as she was tired from the day and finally out of energy. Dante laid her down next to him and fetched a blanket for her. "Like I said before, Alison...you really are something," he whispered.

Alison saw something flying towards her. She looked back and saw the spring she had seen before only this time it was more shallow. All the trees were gone and grass around was as high as her waist. The flying creature came closer until she recognized that it was the dragon. At first she thought he was a different one until he said, "Like you, I have changed. I have shed my skin and have found new flesh...you have grown as well." Alison couldn't believe she was seeing him again and didn't have the same trust as when she first spoke to him.

"Why did I come back here?" she asked the dragon.

"Come back? Alison, you never left," the dragon

replied.

Alison was shocked from his words. "I never told you my name, how did you know?"

The dragon started to spiral up into the air and then looked down at Alison. "I have always been with you, Alison, and never will I abandon you, just remember," the dragon said as it turned its back and flew away.

Once again Alison could hear the words in her mind and could only reply the same way. She yelled back at the dragon through her mind as he drifted away. *"Father…it's you! You're here…you've always been."* Her shout turned into a whisper and then she closed her eyes to hold back her tears. She held them closed for several minutes and when she opened them she was lying on her bed looking straight out her window.

"Dante! Where are you?" she asked out loud. As she realized she was back in her bedroom she jumped off the bed and searched around for Dante. The curtains were moving rapidly from the wind as it released a steady current into the bedroom. The night was quiet and Alison herself was more confused than ever. *"How did I end up back here?"* she wondered.

Once again she searched around her room to find Dante, but he was nowhere around. Alison walked over to the bedroom door and opened it slightly. The creaking from the door made a noisy echo down the corridor. She looked out, but could barely see as the place was dark;

not a single candle was lit in the corridor.

Alison heard footsteps coming her way, footsteps that were all too familiar. She quickly ran to her bed and threw the sheets over her and pretended to be asleep like she used to do. The footsteps came all the way to her door and then stopped suddenly. Everything became quiet again for several moments until finally Alison heard the footsteps walk off into the distance. She then withdrew the sheet from her body and got out of the bed.

She pondered on the situation for several moments trying to make sense of it all. *"It's been days, they must be looking for me, shouldn't they?"* Alison thought. She then began to think maybe her family was glad to get rid of her. Alison couldn't let go of Dante so easily. She stared out her window trying to spot him, but didn't see him or The Majesty anywhere. Alison fell into deep thought and questioned everything. *"Was it even real? This place looks exactly the way I left it...it's like nothing has changed, but I've been gone for weeks. Or have I?"* Alison's mind spiraled in confusion. By now she couldn't tell reality from a dream. *"Maybe this was all in my imagination? Dante...Altaria...everything."*

She had tired her mind with all the thoughts and questions and lay back down in her bed still looking out her window. She closed her eyes as her head rested softly on the pillow. She moved her head around trying to find a comfortable spot, but kept hearing a crunching noise that bothered her. With her hand she could feel some type of parchment under her pillow and to her surprise it was an envelope with a red inked seal plastered on the back of it. Alison was hesitant to open it at first as she was still bewildered on where it came from and from whom. She climbed out of bed and approached the window to use the vast moonlight that beamed through, in order to read the note.

The envelope itself had no name or other markings on the front nor back. She peeled the inked seal off and opened the envelope. She pulled a delicate piece of parchment out that had a border shaped like vines bordering the parchment. Alison laughed out loud when she saw this and that infamous smile returned to her face full of beauty and wonder. "I'll never be too far, Alison, just look up to the sky," Dante said.

She was concentrating on the note so hard that she didn't hear the footsteps outside her room. The door then swung open surprising Alison; she had just enough time to hide the note behind her. Her mother stood in the doorway and gazed straight at Alison who now had a frown on her face, and her mother didn't look too happy either. "I noticed you weren't in your room. I have been looking for you for hours now," her mother said sternly.

Alison stood in silence and wondered, *"Hours?...I have been gone for days... even weeks?"* "I'm sorry mother, I...I don't know what to say."

Her mother looked down at Alison's bare feet which were still covered with dirt. "You know, you're just like your father. Always adventurous and never knowing when to settle down. He knew you had potential and would be great someday," her mother said, and Alison was shocked; she hadn't expected her mother to say such words and a little smile appeared on Alison's face as she was glad to hear her mother felt she was just like her father, great and passionate. Her mother then turned around and Alison only felt her smile stretch further from happiness. Her mother closed the door halfway as she began walking away, but stopped short. "Saphyres is amazing...isn't it?" her mother said.

"What?" Alison asked.

"Oh, nothing," her mother responded as she walked away and closed the door behind her. Alison stood in wonder until a spark from the sky out her window caught her attention. She walked over to her window and once again looked out at the night sky and she could faintly see something flying amongst the stars. It was Dante... Captain of the Skies, but tonight she was Alison of the Skies.

C.C. Cameron is a native of the Sunshine State of Florida (Jacksonville). He has been writing stories since he could pick up a pencil and hasn't stopped since. He has an imagination that is inspired by the children and teens who dream big as well. C.C. has a favorite place he likes to go that he calls his "Imaginative Office," A.K.A Starbucks. That's right! There's something about the smell of fresh coffee and gossiping of Baristas in the background that make it all the fun in the world. In his spare time he enjoys playing badminton and visiting museums across Florida. He writes stories revolving around the adventurous worlds and plots of young characters who are very ambitious. C.C. openly admits that he doesn't read many books and when asked why, he says "because the time I could be reading, I'd rather be writing." And so he does.

CPSIA information can be obtained
at www.ICGtesting.com
Printed in the USA
LVOW11s2229041116
511268LV00005B/6/P

9 780692 800102